FIRE!

Mel screamed. It was a scream that would have done any horror movie victim proud. Everyone in the room jumped and Miss Bitterman ran to her side.

"What is it?" she asked.

"Air," Mel gasped. "The walls are closing in and I think I'm going to suffocate. I have to get out of here."

"Oh dear," Miss Bitterman said, flapping her arms like a frantic bird.

Mel's second scream was, unbelievably, louder than the first.

Seconds later, Miss Bitterman raced back, followed by Mr. Waldo.

Mel's third scream made everyone in the room cover his ears.

With that, a new sound began. It was the bell that signaled a fire alarm.

"Stay right here," Mr. Waldo said.

"And burn? That is definitely illegal," Tess said, heading for the door.

"Cancel it! Cancel the fire alarm!" Mr. Waldo screamed. "Nobody can leave!"

Other Avon Flare Books by
Jane McFann

No Time for Rabbits

FREE THE CONROY SEVEN

JANE McFANN

AN AVON FLARE BOOK

FREE THE CONROY SEVEN is an original publication of Avon Books. This work has never before appeared in book form.

AVON BOOKS
A division of
The Hearst Corporation
1350 Avenue of the Americas
New York, New York 10019

Copyright © 1993 by Jane McFann
Published by arrangement with the author
Library of Congress Catalog Card Number: 92-93925
ISBN: 0-380-76401-6
RL: 5.4

First Avon Flare Printing: April 1993

AVON TRADEMARK REG. U.S. PAT. OFF. AND IN OTHER COUNTRIES, MARCA REGISTRADA, HECHO EN CANADA

Printed in Canada

UNV 10 9 8 7 6 5 4 3 2

To my parents, whose love and support get me through the bad times and enrich the good times.

To my colleagues at Glasgow High School, who are constant sources of friendship, knowledge, and inspiration.

And to my agent, Linda Allen, whose encouragement never runs out.

Chapter 1

"May I have your attention, please? May I have your attention, please!" The hyper voice of Mr. Waldo, Conroy High School's assistant principal, interrupted every second period class in the building. Lessons, conversations, debates, arguments, band rehearsals, and everything else came to a grudging halt.

"This is Mr. Waldo, your assistant principal." As if it were necessary to announce that. His voice, almost an octave higher than any other man's in the building, was distinctive beyond doubt.

"There is a matter of grave urgency in our building at this moment." That stilled the remaining talkers.

"It's World War Three! The bombs have been fired! We're all going to die!" That was the senior class clown's voice booming out of an English class on the second floor. Laughter followed, but it was decidedly nervous laughter.

"Is it really the end of the world?" one tentative voice asked.

"Of course not," the teacher answered, glaring but then turning to look at the intercom speaker in the ceiling, waiting for Mr. Waldo's explanation. Unfortunately, none was forthcoming.

"I want every teacher in the building to make a list of every student presently not in class. This includes students who have been given passes out of class for any reason."

"It'd be easier to list who is present," grumbled a ninth grade teacher whose students were perennially absent.

"I repeat, I want a list of all missing students. Have it in my office within five minutes. Thank you for your cooperation. This is Mr. Waldo. Continue with the educational process."

"Yeah, let's process," a girl said.

"How about if you process this list down to Mr. Waldo's office for me," her teacher said.

"But I want to take it. Let me take it," a boy yelled.

"No, she said I could," the girl said, grabbing the list and dashing for the door.

The boy started after her. "Sit," the teacher barked.

The boy promptly sat. "Good senior," the teacher said. "Remember that without a passing grade in this class, you don't graduate in June."

"Yes, ma'am," the boy said meekly. "I'm ready to learn now, ma'am." With a laugh, the class resumed.

"May I have your attention, please? May I have your attention, please. This is Mr. Waldo, your assistant principal." It was no more that ten minutes later when second period was once again interrupted.

"I am dismayed at the frivolous attitudes of some of our students—at least I am assuming that it is the work of students and not of our esteemed faculty members." Mr. Waldo's voice had done the seemingly impossible and risen even higher in pitch.

"It seems that some of our messengers have made additions to the lists of missing students." His voice was now trembling with anger. "I do not believe that Frank Zappa, Jim Morrison, Donald Duck, Richard Nixon, Batman, or Jon Bon Jovi are presently en-

2

rolled in this school. In the name of accuracy in this matter of grave importance, I want each teacher to make a new list of all students missing from class. I will pick them up personally. Thank you, and continue with ... continue with ... whatever."

By this time, laughter was echoing off the hallways of Conroy High. It had barely quieted down by the time Mr. Waldo's trotting footsteps were heard. Door by door, hallway by hallway, floor by floor, his apoplectic face appeared. Thinning brown hair was combed from a part near his left ear and crossed all the way over to the right ear. His rapid pace, however, had loosened some of these strands, and they were flying back wildly. His face was an unhealthy shade of red, and his eyes bulged. A vein in his temple pulsed ominously, and one eyebrow twitched. He snatched the list out of each teacher's hand with an abrupt thank you and then sped off, tie bouncing on his bony chest.

Mr. Waldo, assistant principal, certainly did not appear to be a happy camper.

Chapter 2

It was five minutes into third period when Mr. Waldo's next announcement interrupted the "educational process."

"May I have your attention, please? May I have your attention, please. This is Mr. Waldo, your assistant principal." He didn't sound much calmer than he had the last time. "I would like the following students to report to my office immediately. Do not, I repeat, do NOT try to evade me. According to my computer records, you were in homeroom but were not in second period class. I am certain I am correct in assuming that you are still in the building, and I want you in my office immediately. If necessary, I will track you down personally, so please come willingly."

Students laughed. "This sounds like the wild West. Waldo the tracker: scourge of the scoundrels," a girl with wildly teased hair said.

"Don't laugh," said a boy in the back row. "I bet you money you're on the list."

"You're so lame," the girl retorted. "I was in second period. You saw me."

"Did not. In fact, I even reminded the teacher to put your name on the list."

"You lie. You know I was there."

"Sorry. The whole class commented to the teacher that it certainly was quiet without you there."

"Shut up. Mr. Waldo's giving the names."

"Marcus Duke," Mr. Waldo intoned.

"Come on down!" the back-row boy yelled in his best *The Price Is Right* imitation.

"Tess Eisman," Mr. Waldo said.

"Tess? Brain of the senior class?" the teacher asked in amazement.

"Melissa Savage," Mr. Waldo announced, a tremor in his voice.

"You can savage me anytime, Melissa," a muscle-shirted boy lounging on the windowsill said.

"Shut up, sleazeball," his supposed girlfriend whined.

"Julian Thompson," Mr. Waldo continued.

"Oooh," the class chorused, surprise in their voices.

"Megan Massapalo," the voice continued.

"Mr. Waldo has gone over the edge," a girl with a tatoo on her shoulder said in amazement. "I've gone to school with Megan since first grade, and she's never even gotten detention. I mean, she hardly even talks."

"Maybe you should hang around her more," someone said sarcastically.

"Chad Rheingard," Mr. Waldo said.

"You're right. Mr. Waldo is wacko this time."

"The final name on the list," Mr. Waldo announced, pausing dramatically, "is Eddie Broncoman."

Laughter came from the class as they all wheeled to face Eddie.

"What is this crap?" Eddie screamed, bounding to his feet.

"You're supposed to report to Mr. Waldo's office immediately," his teacher said, shaking his head.

"I was in my second period class," Eddie screamed. He looked around the room, his eyes stopping on a boy in the back row. "Hey, Slimeball, wasn't I in class last period?"

"I don't remember," Slimeball answered.

"Wake up," Eddie yelled, running back to hover in front of the unfortunate Slimeball, who had lived with that nickname since first grade. "I was there. We read some story about a guy who pushes a rock up a mountain and then it falls down again."

"Huh?" Slimeball said, shaking his head.

"I was there," Eddie said.

"Mr. Waldo awaits you," the teacher said calmly.

"Well he can wait until hell freezes over because I'm not going," Eddie said, throwing himself back down in his seat.

"Just explain to him that there must be a mistake. I'm sure it's easy to solve."

"Not going," Eddie mumbled.

"He'll track you down," the teacher said.

The class promptly started singing the shark theme from *Jaws*.

"I'll hide," Eddie said, slumping down in his seat. "I hate that man."

The class laughed again; after all, Eddie was about 6′ 3″ tall, and hiding was a little difficult in a student desk he barely fit into in the first place.

"Eddie," the teacher said again.

"No," Eddie said.

"Eddie," the teacher said with growing emphasis.

"Why me?" Eddie asked plaintively.

"Could it be the fact that you slit the tires on Mr. Waldo's car?" a classmate asked delicately.

"That was in ninth grade after he suspended me for

smoking in the bathroom," Eddie said, as if that justified it.

"Or could it be because you called him an old fart?" someone else asked.

"That was in tenth grade, and besides, he *is* an old . . ."

"Eddie, it's time for you to go now," the teacher said firmly.

Mumbling and stomping his feet, Eddie made his way to the door.

"This isn't fair," he said.

"We're behind you," the girl who had been sitting next to him said. Then, using his nickname, she began to chant. "Bronco, Bronco, Bronco." The chant was picked up by the whole class until the room resounded with his name.

Eddie listened for a few more rounds, then clasped his hands over his head, bowing like a prize fighter about to enter the ring. "I'll be back," he announced, then flung open the door dramatically.

"Bronco, Bronco, Bronco." The chant faded as he disappeared down the hallway toward the waiting Mr. Waldo.

Chapter 3

The first person Eddie Broncoman ran into as he approached Mr. Waldo's office was Marcus Duke.

"This is a beat scene," Marcus announced, flinging back his hair, which was short in the back but with long, straight bangs that hung into his eyes.

"I can think of other words," Bronco said, falling into step beside Marcus.

"Mr. Waldo is prejudiced against skaters," Marcus said. "He's a definite peon."

"Skaters?" Bronco asked. "What are you, one of those ice dancers or something?"

"Skateboards are my life, man. You should try it sometime. There's a ramp near the university campus that is way cool."

"Way cool," Bronco repeated, shaking his head. "Right now I'd like to way cool Waldo."

"Do you believe he banned skateboards from school? All these great halls and walls and stairs—what a waste."

"Why do you think we're being called down?" Bronco asked as they approached Mr. Waldo's office.

"Look, man, Trig class was a beat scene so I cut. I didn't think he'd broadcast it all over the building."

"I went to class and I still got called down," Bronco said.

"Beat scene, man," Marcus said, shaking his head sadly.

They both entered the Main Office, where the head secretary pointed toward the hallway that led to more offices. They went past the closed door of the principal's office, then arrived at another suite of offices.

"How did she know who we were?" Marcus asked.

"Every time I walk in, they send me straight to one administrator or another," Eddie said. "One time the pay phone was trashed, and I just needed to use the office phone to call my mother to tell her to bring my gym clothes, and that woman out there still sent me to the principal."

"Definitely uncool," Marcus said. "What happened?"

"I used his phone," Eddie said, "and he gave me detention because he said he'd seen me in the vicinity too often. I hate this place. I swear I'm going to blow it up."

"You swear what? What did you just say? Repeat that. Repeat that right now." Mr. Waldo popped out from behind a closed door and jumped into the path of Marcus and Bronco.

"I said I swear I'm going to blow up if I don't get to a bathroom soon. Must have been those nachos and beer last night," Bronco said, glaring at Mr. Waldo.

"I'll thank you not to discuss such nasty matters in my presence," Mr. Waldo said with a snort.

"Then don't ask me to repeat conversations that didn't involve you in the first place," Eddie retorted.

"Chill, man," Marcus said quietly.

"I've got your number, young man," Mr. Waldo said, stabbing his finger in Bronco's chest. "You'll pay for the years of torment you've given me."

Bronco seemed to levitate off the ground as he loomed over Mr. Waldo.

"Take a seat in here," Mr. Waldo said, turning on his heel and going back through the door. He waited, tapping his foot impatiently, while Bronco shook his head and Marcus nudged him forward. They entered a good sized conference room with a large wooden table surrounded by fifteen or so large chairs with padded arms.

"Sit," Mr. Waldo said. Both boys stared at him.

"Sit," Mr. Waldo repeated, the blood vessel at his temple visibly pulsing again.

Bronco stared straight at him and barked.

"What did you just do?" Mr. Waldo sputtered. "How dare you bark at me?"

"Treat me like a dog and I'll act like one," Bronco said.

"This could be a trip," Marcus said, pulling out a chair, throwing himself into it, and propping his feet up on the table.

"Get your feet off that table," Mr. Waldo said, turning away from Bronco, who was now growling softly. "Would you do that to your mother's furniture at home?"

"Yes," Marcus answered. Bronco growled louder in approval.

"Miss Bitterman," Mr. Waldo yelled. "Miss Bitterman, come here." Bronco growled more ominously. "Please," Mr. Waldo added, with a glance at Bronco.

"Yes, Mr. Waldo?" Miss Bitterman fluttered in from an adjoining cubbyhole that seemed to be her office. Her bright orange hair glowed around her head in a frizzy halo, her bangs covering the top part of her horn-rimmed glasses. She looked to be thirty or maybe forty. It was hard to pin down an age since

10

her hair hid most of her face, her thick glasses distorted a clear view of her eyes, and her body was covered by a shapeless, drop-waisted dress.

"See to it that these two don't go anywhere."

Bronco walked over to stand beside Miss Bitterman. He had over a foot's worth of height advantage.

"Hello, dear," she said.

"Hi, honey," Bronco answered.

Mr. Waldo sputtered bursts of undecipherable consonants as he stormed through a second door into what must be his office.

"What have you done this time?" Miss Bitterman asked Bronco.

"Nothing," he said.

Marcus recrossed his legs on the table and leaned back to watch.

"Is this Mr. Waldo's office?" a throaty voice asked from the entrance to the room.

Marcus turned around, nearly tipping over his chair when he saw the origin of the voice.

"This is definitely way cool," he said with a big smile.

Chapter 4

"Are you part of this Waldo scene?" Marcus asked hopefully, swinging his feet off the table to get a better angle on the vision at the doorway.

"Sure," the deep, sexy voice answered. "Nobody leaves me out, now do they?" She undulated toward Marcus, hips swiveling.

"Cut the crap, Melissa," Bronco said.

"Mel," the girl said with only a trace of hesitation. "Melissa is just too . . . sweet and innocent, if you know what I mean."

"You know her?" Marcus asked Bronco with a touch of admiration.

"Unfortunately," Bronco answered.

"Oh, Eddie, now how long are you going to sulk? Just because I wouldn't go to the prom with you. You have to understand that the quarterback asked me, and the soccer team captain, and then there was that college guy that I was seeing at the frat parties on campus . . . well, you know how it is." She flipped her dark hair behind her shoulder and gave Bronco a smile and a wink.

"Best thing that ever happened to me," Bronco said. "Ruin my reputation to be seen with a girl like you. I was only a junior then—didn't know any better."

"And what do you know now?" Mel said, flowing over to stand behind Bronco.

"Enough to stay away from stuck-up, two-timing teases like you," Bronco snarled.

"Now you just know you don't mean that," Mel purred, reaching her hands out to rest them on Bronco's shoulders. Bronco jerked away as if he had accidentally touched an electrified fence.

"Don't touch me," Bronco snarled. "I might get something."

"Bronco, beat scene, man," Marcus interrupted. "All this arguing is making me tense." He rolled his shoulders and twisted his head from side to side, wincing with pain.

Mel turned away from Bronco and strolled to Marcus, glancing back once to make sure that Bronco's eyes were following her swaying posterior. They were, she noticed with a smug smile. "Here, let me help," she said, beginning to massage the shoulders of an accommodating Marcus, who leaned back to give her more access. Mel's collection of silver bangle bracelets jangled, and her black miniskirt rode a little higher up her perfect thighs. The black, scoop-necked leotard coated her chest.

"Another hour or two of this and I'll be way cool," Marcus purred. Bronco growled from across the table.

"I have arrived. You may now begin." The voice from the doorway interrupted Marcus' neck massage, and all three checked the source of the voice.

Horn-rimmed glasses adorned a handsome black face, and a tall, lean body posed in the doorway. "Come on in," Mel invited, as if she were hosting a party in her own home.

"And what is the occasion for this gathering?" the newcomer asked.

"Beats me," Bronco said. "Aren't you Julie somebody?"

"Julian Bond Thompson," he answered, enunciating each syllable clearly and slowly. "Remember that name. You'll be hearing plenty of it in the future."

"I'm Mel Savage." Her voice was flirtatious; after all, this was a male, wasn't it? Mel never missed a chance to enhance her image as reigning Conroy High sex kitten.

"Marcus Duke, Skate Posse Summer Tour of Love," Marcus said, getting up to shake Julian's hand.

"Pleased to make your acquaintance," Julian said, immediately walking to the head of the table and taking a seat. He leaned back slightly, crossed his hands, and looked down either side of the large table. Bronco was slumped in a chair partway down one side, eyes narrowed into slits. Marcus had returned to a seat on the other side, his feet once again up on the table. Mel had chosen to sit next to Marcus, turning her chair so that she was angled into his legs. One of her hands rested casually on his calf.

"Now, what is our order of business today?" Marcus asked calmly.

With that, Mr. Waldo burst into the room from his office. "Are they all here?" he screamed into Miss Bitterman's general vicinity. Her head popped out of her office and into the room.

"One, two, three, four, five," she counted, pointing around the table. "There are five students here." For a moment she sounded like a first grade teacher.

Marcus, Mel, Bronco, and Julian looked at her with matching puzzled faces. Then they looked to the far end of the table nearest to the door. There sat a girl who must have slipped into the room just as Mr. Waldo had captured their attention. She was motionless, long light-brown hair nearly hiding her face, which was averted from the rest. She was so still it didn't even seem like she was breathing.

"How'd she get in here?" Bronco asked in amazement.

"I want two more," Mr. Waldo bellowed. "There are seven students on my list, and I want them all. ALL!"

"Yes, Mr. Waldo," Miss Bitterman said, her hands fluttering up to her hair, patting at it futilely. "Seven. Two are missing."

"Want me to go find them for you?" Bronco asked helpfully.

"Why, Eddie, how nice of you to offer," Miss Bitterman said, smiling at him.

"Don't you move," Mr. Waldo said, his voice a hiss rather than a holler. "You're not leaving this room until I say so, and that may be a long say so."

"What's a long say so?" Bronco asked, brow wrinkled in puzzlement, leaning across the table toward Marcus.

"Maybe a day or two," Marcus whispered.

"A day or two?" Bronco bellowed. "No way can that man keep me here a day or two. That's illegal. I'll break down the door. I'll . . . I'll pee on his carpet. No way can that . . ."

"Silence," Mr. Waldo yelled. "I don't want to hear one syllable from any one of you. Do you understand me? Silence. Miss Bitterman, don't let them talk." With that, Mr. Waldo slammed back into his office.

"But Mr. Waldo," Miss Bitterman said to the closed door. "How am I supposed to . . ."

"Julian Thompson. Perhaps I can be of service to you." Julian got up, went to where Miss Bitterman was still talking to the closed door, and held out a hand for her to shake.

15

"You're not supposed to talk," she said.

"My good lady, does this make sense to you?" Julian's calm words seemed to have little impact on her.

"Mr. Waldo wants you to be silent," she persisted.

"Why?" Julian asked quietly.

"Because . . . because . . . because he said so," she finally answered.

With that, Bronco raised his hand. "Yes, Eddie?" Miss Bitterman said, seeming relieved to have a reason not to pursue her conversation with Julian.

"I have to go to the bathroom," Bronco said plaintively.

"Oh, my," Miss Bitterman said, hands fluttering again. "Can't you just hold it in for awhile, dear?"

"No," Bronco said.

"What's going on here?" a new voice asked from the doorway. "I really don't have time for this foolishness."

Chapter 5

"Mr. Waldo wants to see you," Miss Bitterman said nervously. "That is, he wants to see you if your name was called. Is your name on that list?"

"My name is Tess Eisman," the composed young lady announced.

"Yes, indeed, you're on the list," Miss Bitterman said. "You'd better have a seat. And be quiet, please."

Tess stared at the assembled group and then shook her head in disgust. "I really don't have time for this," she said again.

"Tess, good to see you," Julian said from the head of the table.

"Are you behind this, Julian?" Tess asked icily.

"Whatever could you mean?" Julian asked, bringing his fingers together as if forming a steeple with them.

"Are you trying to keep me out of Calculus class so that your average can creep that tenth of a percentage point higher than mine and you will be valedictorian rather than me?"

"Tess, Tess, Tess. How could you even conceive of such a plan?"

"Cut the crap, Julian."

"Wow, man. I didn't know you knew words like that." Marcus was looking at Tess in amazement.

"I know more words than anyone in the senior class," Tess said with a shrug. "If you don't believe me, check my verbal score on the SAT. It's higher than Julian's by forty points."

"That's because those tests are socially and racially biased," Julian said with rising volume.

"Right, Julian. You grew up two houses down the street from me," Tess answered, with not a degree of warmth in her voice.

"What's a valedictorian?" Bronco asked.

"Top grade point average in the graduating class," Marcus explained. Tess and Julian wheeled on Bronco with mouths slightly dropped in amazement.

"Sorry," Bronco said in sarcastic apology. "It was never much of a concern in my life, you know? I'm about as likely to get good grades as I am to get AIDS, you know what I mean?"

"You could get AIDS," Mel said, causing the attention to shift to her.

"I could not," Bronco protested vehemently. "What are you saying, I'm gay? You better not be saying that, you little tramp."

"Chill, man," Marcus said, ever in quest of peace. "You could get it from mosquitoes."

"Gay mosquitoes?" Bronco yelled. "Gay mosquitoes can give me AIDS?"

"You're wrong about mosquitoes, homosexual or otherwise," Tess said. "There is absolutely no evidence that AIDS is spread by mosquitoes. It's spread by sexual activities, sharing needles, blood transfusions, babies getting it from their mothers before birth. Not mosquitoes."

"Toilet seats?" Bronco asked.

"No," Tess replied.

"Then I'm not getting it."

"Do you know," Mel said, her hand having now moved up to Marcus' thigh, "that when you have sex with someone, medically speaking, you're having sex with everyone that person has ever had sex with? Isn't that amazing?"

"Thank God I didn't go to the prom with you," Bronco said.

"I can't stay here any longer," Tess announced.

"Afraid of missing Calculus?" Julian asked with an edge to his words.

"Quiet!" Mr. Waldo screamed, throwing open his door again. "Doesn't anyone here understand the English language any longer? Miss Bitterman!"

Miss Bitterman's door opened cautiously, and she peeked out.

"How are you going to keep these students quiet if your door is closed? Get out here where you can do your job."

"But I was doing my job in my office where I have my typewriter and my phone and my filing cabinet," Miss Bitterman said quietly but somewhat firmly.

"Bring them in here," Mr. Waldo snapped.

"Excuse me?" she said.

"Do I have to do everything around here?" Mr. Waldo said peevishly. He stomped to Miss Bitterman's door and flung it open the rest of the way. Then he grabbed the edge of her desk and pulled. Nothing happened. He braced his feet, grabbed the edge of the desk, and pulled again. The desk moved maybe an inch and a half.

"Help me, Miss Bitterman," Mr. Waldo hissed through clenched teeth.

Miss Bitterman went to the far side of her desk and pushed. She was surprisingly strong for her size, because the desk moved a good foot and nearly tripped Mr. Waldo.

"Eddie, dear, why don't you help us?" Miss Bitterman asked Bronco.

"Because I have to go to the bathroom," Bronco replied.

"Oh, yes, I forgot about that," she said, hunching down to shove again.

By the time the desk was moved to the doorway, sweat was dripping down Mr. Waldo's forehead. The doorway proved to be a major obstacle. The desk must have gone through the doorway on its side, because it sure wouldn't fit when it was upright. The best Mr. Waldo and Miss Bitterman could do was to wedge it firmly in the door frame with one corner angled out.

Mr. Waldo had to have heard the snickers coming from the table where the students were sitting. "Fine," he said. "Now you can keep your eye on them." He wheeled back toward his office. "Quiet," he said once again.

"Sir?" Julian asked politely.

"What?" Mr. Waldo snapped.

"Could you please tell us why we're gathered here?"

"When I'm good and ready to," Mr. Waldo bellowed.

"Mr. Waldo, I'm sure you have your reasons, but I believe that the Student Code of Conduct specifies that students have the right to know why they are taken out of class," Julian said politely.

"Let me tell you something," Mr. Waldo said with a quiver in his voice. "You're smart, but you're not quite as smart as you think. You're not ranked second in your class. You're third."

"Ah hah," Tess laughed.

"And you, young lady, you're not number one," Mr. Waldo announced, slamming his door triumphantly behind him.

"Ah hah," Julian said, his laugh a mocking imitation of Tess'. "I thought you had a 4.0."

"I do," Tess said, "in every way that counts."

"Not according to Mr. Waldo," Julian said, leaning back in his chair.

"All right, I admit I got a B in Gym in ninth grade, but that shouldn't count," Tess said petulantly.

"But it does," Julian said.

"Well, Mr. Hot Shot, what about you?" Tess asked.

"A B in ninth grade in Exploratory Shop," Julian admitted grudgingly.

"And since Gym is only half a credit and Shop is a full credit, my grade point average is higher than yours," Tess said triumphantly. Then her face fell.

"Someone must have a 4.0," Julian and Tess groaned simultaneously.

"This is sick," Bronco announced. "We're all teenagers. We're supposed to be thinking about sex, drugs, and rock and roll. These two weirdos are thinking about grades. I'm on the wrong list. I don't belong anywhere near you two."

"Well, I think about one of those three a lot," Mel purred.

"You do more than think about it, from what I hear," Bronco snapped.

"Jealous?" Mel asked, flipping her hair over her shoulder and sticking out her chest in the process.

Miss Bitterman's mouth was hanging open as she listened to all of this. "Young people," she said. They gave no sign of having heard her. She tried to get out into the room but her desk had her trapped. "Young people," she said more loudly.

"You got a problem?" Bronco snapped, his mood obviously getting worse by the minute.

"Well, Eddie, yes, I do, now that you mention it. I seem to be trapped in here."

"Stay there," Bronco said. "You don't want to be out here with these weirdos."

"Yes, Eddie, but Mr. Waldo wants me to keep you quiet," Miss Bitterman protested.

"Mr. Waldo is a ..." Bronco was cut off by Mr. Waldo himself who came out of his office so fast that he must have been ejected from his chair. Actually, he must have had his ear against the door.

"What? What did you say? Mr. Waldo is a what?" The assistant principal was a shade of red that went past ripe tomato into some new realm of intensity.

"Sorry I'm late," said a cheerful voice at the outer doorway, accompanied by an electrical whirring sound. "I had to wait until someone got the elevator key." The whirring sound continued as the source of the voice steered his electric wheelchair into the room. "I'm Chad Rheingard," he announced, positioning himself near the girl with the long brown hair who still hadn't spoken or, for that matter, even looked up.

Chapter 6

"You're Chad Rheingard?" Mr. Waldo asked.

"Yes, I am," Chad answered cheerfully.

"I'm sorry, but there must be some mistake."

"No, I really am Chad Rheingard."

"I mean with the names on my list. Obviously your name must have been on it in error. You may go, young man."

"Oh no you don't," Chad said with surprising vehemence. "My name was on that list, and you can't kick me off of it because I'm handicapped. That's discrimination."

"Let him stay and I'll go," Bronco said, getting out of his seat.

"No," Mr. Waldo barked. "Look, Chad, it's not discrimination; I've obviously simply put your name on the list by mistake. I'm sure that you were in your second period class."

"No, I wasn't," Chad said with what almost sounded like pride.

"You must have been excused with a pass then," Mr. Waldo said, a confused look crossing his face.

"Nope," Chad said smugly. "I cut."

"Look here," Mr. Waldo said. "I still made a mistake with your inclusion. You're free to go back to class."

"If cutting gets your name on the list then I cut and I deserve to be on the list and I'm staying," Chad said firmly. He looked around the room. "This is great," he said. "Hi." He smiled at the rest of the students, who were staring at him in amazement.

"Now just hold on here," Bronco said with the volume of his voice rising on every syllable. "Chad cuts class, and you want to let him go. I went to my second period class, and you won't even let me go to the bathroom. Now that's discrimination!"

Mr. Waldo must have sensed that he was losing control of the situation. He shook himself like a wet dog, straightened his tie, and spoke in a loud and firm voice. He was obviously making an effort to take the squeak out of it because the result sounded fake, like a bad actor trying to sound dignified. "Now that you are all here, we may begin," he intoned. "Someone in this room has information that I want."

"Ah, so we're not here to be given a scholarship or an award, then, are we?" Julian said, sounding disappointed.

"Not exactly," Mr. Waldo said, then resumed his speech. "Although what has been done is an extremely serious offense, I will consider showing a slight degree of lenience if a full and rapid confession is forthcoming."

"Bronco, what did you do now?" Mel asked with a snort.

"I'm innocent," he protested.

"You're about as innocent as I am," she said with a coy smile.

"Stop it!" Mr. Waldo yelled, his voice leaping up again. "Stop it right now," he said, this time remembering to lower his voice. "I want answers, and I want them right now. Do you understand?"

"Excuse me, Mr. Waldo, but what is the question?" Julian was again the speaker.

"One of you knows the question and the answer," Mr. Waldo intoned mysteriously.

"Yes, but what about the rest of us? You're wasting our time," Tess said impatiently.

"Miss Bitterman," Mr. Waldo called, ignoring Tess. "Miss Bitterman, give each of these students a sheet of paper and a writing utensil."

Miss Bitterman looked at him in amazement; after all, she was trapped in her office by her desk. "Mr. Waldo," she began.

"Quickly, Miss Bitterman," Mr. Waldo said.

Poor Miss Bitterman grabbed a handful of pens and pencils out of the container on her desk, picked up a pad of paper, and, as gracefully as possible, climbed up on her desk, walked over it, and descended the other side. Then she scurried around the table, handing out supplies.

"Now," Mr. Waldo said firmly, "I want each of you to write down everything you know about today's events. Be sure to sign your name. Remember, I will find out the truth anyway, but you can make it easier on yourself with a full and honest confession."

"This is absurd," Tess said, throwing down her pen.

"You have twenty minutes," Mr. Waldo said, looking carefully at his watch.

"That's the question—everything we know about today?" Bronco asked in amazement.

"Yes," Mr. Waldo said. "And if anyone chooses not to answer, I will assume that there is a guilty conscience behind it."

Tess reached over and retrieved the pen. She glanced down the table at Julian, who was already

25

writing. Seeing his pen flowing over the paper seemed to motivate her, and she bent to her work. Eventually, so did the others. Mr. Waldo went into his office, and Miss Bitterman sat on the edge of her desk and tried to swing her legs around to the other side inconspicuously. It didn't work, and she had to slide across on her bottom, pushing over the telephone in the process. After that, silence descended on the room for the first time, marred only by the sounds of pens and pencils crossing paper.

In exactly twenty minutes, Mr. Waldo reentered and walked around the room, retrieving each paper, checking to make sure it had a name on it. Then he went back to his office to read the results.

In the interest of complying with your request, I will now narrate to you what I know of today's events. This is difficult to perform to my normal high standards since I am not cognizant of the information you are seeking; hence, I may not be able to focus as tightly as I would like to on a well-supported answer. Nevertheless, I will do my best; after all, you are an administrator and as such hold substantial power to influence my future.

I arrived at Conroy High School in ample time to attend homeroom and my first period class. I was unavoidably detained from my second period class; I am certain you understand that occasionally academic needs arise which must be met in a slightly unorthodox manner. You will note, however, that I answered your summons promptly; I am desirous of cooperating with you as fully as possible.

I would like to take this opportunity to compliment you on the way you carry out your duties, and since you are such a competent and concerned educator, I would like to present to you an injustice which I am certain that, if made aware of, you would work to resolve. That injustice is the current practice of allowing elective courses to count in the calculation of grade point averages. The measure of academic excellence should be based on academic courses; a student who excels in calculus, physics, and many other challenging subjects should not be penalized because of a few ninth grade slips with a band saw, now should he?

I eagerly await your response; I am certain you will give my complaint the full and measured consideration it merits.

Julian Thompson

What is this, English class again? I already went to English class today, second period as a matter of fact, you seem to be ignoring that fact. Well, I want you to know that I did nothing wrong today and your being unfair to me again, like you have been other times when you never listen to my side of the story. Like those tires. Just because someone saw me out in the parking lot, and just because I had an ice pick in my pocket when you searched me doesn't mean that I was the one who did it. There are lots of reasons why someone would carry an ice pick. Like opened up clogged bottles of glue. Or separating Life Savers that got melted together in the roll. Lots of reasons. And maybe I was out in the parking lot because my grandmother was sick and I needed to go to the hospital to see her. Yeah, thats the reason. But would you listen to me? No. Well today I been a perfect student. As long as you don't count that spitball that I threw at Grant but missed and it accidentally hit my English teacher but I can't believe you heard about that one already and besides it wasn't even a very wet spitball.

If that's what this is all about, I confess. I threw a spitball at Grant and hit the teacher by mistake and you said you'd take it easy if we confessed. Well, I confess already.

Eddie BRONCO Broncoman
P. S. Now can I go to the bathroom?

I suppose that I am here wasting my time because I did not attend my second period class today. That problem is yours, not mine. If you'd hire a competent teacher to teach honors twelfth grade physics, then I'd attend more regularly. As it is, I know more than he does, and I'm insulted to sit there and absorb useless knowledge when all that he knows and more is in the textbook.

I consider myself not merely a student, but a scholar, and I feel you have a responsibility to meet my needs. I also must admit that I find it difficult to imagine that there is a student unknown to me who has a better grade point average than I. Who is it?

Tess Eisman
P. S. Is it necessary to remind you that my father is a lawyer? Surely it won't come to that.

This is great! I've been in this school for four years and I never got in trouble before. I think it is because I am handicapped and people are prejudiced against handicapped people and think that they can never do anything wrong. Well they can! Thank you for giving me a chance to show that.

I hope you can read this. I have to print, but at home I use a computer.

Chad Rheingard

Today has been a really crummy day for me. It started when the left side of my hair just wouldn't curl right. I had to do it three times before it was perfect, and by that time I didn't have time to eat breakfast. That's okay, though, because I want to lose about five pounds. Everyone says that I'm crazy to want to lose weight because my body's perfect the way it is, but I still think five pounds less would be even better. Then John Grant, that fox in the senior class who wrestles, was supposed to give me a ride to school but he forgot, which I simply can't imagine. Anyway, Rich drove by and I waved to him and he stopped and gave me a ride so I was only a few minutes late for homeroom.

Then in first period the teacher gave a pop quiz, which I think should be outlawed when we're seniors (RAH!!!!!) and then after I finished I was putting on my mascara which in my rush this morning I had forgotten and I couldn't go any longer without it, and that teacher TOOK AWAY MY MASCARA!!!!! Can you believe that? I hate that woman!!!! You should get rid of her.

Then second period I had personal problems (girl stuff, you know)—do you really want me to go into detail?!?!? No, I didn't think so!! Then I got called down here, and I'm sure you'll let us out in time for lunch, won't you?

The guys would be really bored if I wasn't there!!!!!

Mel Savage

Skaters are misunderstood. All I want to do is get out of this school and begin my Skate Posse Summer Tour of Love. There are some groovy ramps down at the beach, and plenty of parties and chicks who see that skaters are the heroes of love, peace, and the ultimate quest for fun.

This is a beat scene, and you're interrupting my flow. Besides, I don't like to use words. If you want to understand me, then watch me on my board where my moves will let you see the essence of my soul. Maybe you'd even like to help sponsor our Summer Tour of Love. We're a little short of bread.

My goal in life is to grow the hair on my toes long enough to braid.

If love is the answer, then all other questions are irrelevant. (That includes yours!)

If life is a bitch, then I don't plan on being a hydrant.

Skate till your shins splint.

Marcus Duke

What is today
a wisp of taffeta
over my grandmother's petticoat
a glimmer of moonlight
seen through a dream
a shimmering tear
locked in my heart

What is today
if the taffeta tears

30

and the moon doesn't rise
and my heart is locked
in a past full of pain
and a day where no sun
warms my shivering soul

Megan Massapalo

Chapter 7

The students let the silence linger; in fact, it was unnatural how quiet the room remained. That spell was broken a few minutes later, however, when Mr. Waldo erupted from his office again.

"Miss Bitterman, in my office please."

"Yes, Mr. Waldo." This time she tried a small leap onto the desk top that left her in a crouched position, and she duck-walked to the edge and jumped down.

She smiled feebly at the students, then entered the office.

"Shut the door, Miss Bitterman," came Mr. Waldo's exasperated voice. With one last look at the assembled quiet students, Miss Bitterman shut the door.

Bronco promptly lumbered to the door and leaned his ear against it. The others stared at him in amazement.

"Miss Bitterman, you seem to have some insight into these heathens."

"They're not really heathens, Mr. Waldo. They're a little ornery at times, but they're not really bad kids."

"Ornery? After what has happened today, you say they're ornery?"

"Well, maybe a little worse than ornery," Miss Bitterman said tentatively.

"You're the one who brought this . . . this situation to my attention, Miss Bitterman, so surely you know the magnitude of the problem."

"Well, you know that you sent me to the Central Administration Offices to pick up those forms for you, and when I got back here to school, I couldn't help but notice. I'm sorry if I've upset you."

"Upset? Of course I'm upset. But I'm glad it was you who noticed. Lord knows if others find out, my credibility . . ." Mr. Waldo began sputtering and coughing.

"Mr. Waldo, please try to calm yourself. You know how stress makes your stomach flare up."

"I'll calm myself when I know who the ruffian is who is responsible. Look at these papers. Just look at them! I've read every one of them, and I can't find a single clue. It has to be one of them, and I'm going to find out which one and prosecute his or her little body right out of this building."

"Now, Mr. Waldo, it might be someone else. Maybe it was a stranger, or a kid from another school, or someone who cut school and isn't in the building at all right now. Maybe you should just call maintenance, get them over here, and let those kids go back to class."

"Are you crazy, Miss Bitterman? Let them go? It's one of them. I know it, I can feel it, and I'm going to get the little bush-league criminal if it's the last thing I do."

"Now Mr. Waldo, try to . . ."

"Read these." Mr. Waldo threw the papers down on the desk in front of Miss Bitterman, who sat opposite him.

The first one she read was Tess Eisman's. "Uh oh," she said. "Her father is a lawyer. Maybe you should let her go before she demands to make a phone call."

"You think I'm going to be intimidated by that? Besides, she's too concerned about her class rank to cross me," Mr. Waldo said smugly. "She's already been in five times this year to check on it. See anything else?"

"No," Miss Bitterman said, going on to Eddie's paper.

"That boy's nothing but trouble," Mr. Waldo said.

"But he was in class second period," Miss Bitterman protested.

"I don't care. He's sneaky," Mr. Waldo said.

"I think you'd better let him go to the bathroom," Miss Bitterman said gently.

"I hope his kidneys burst," Mr. Waldo said savagely.

"Now calm yourself," Miss Bitterman said with a worried look on her face. "This job isn't worth the stress you're putting yourself under."

"Keep reading," Mr. Waldo insisted.

"My, my, this Juilian writes like a college professor," Miss Bitterman commented after finishing another paper.

"Overuse of the semicolon," Mr. Waldo huffed.

Miss Bitterman read the next paper in the stack and giggled.

"What?" Mr. Waldo snapped.

"Mel Savage. I'd forgotten what it's like to be young and flirtatious."

"And think that every male on the face of the Earth is in love with you? Foolish girl. Besides, she's not even that attractive."

"You really don't think so?"

"Not my type. Too flashy and . . . tawdry, if you know what I mean."

"What is your type, Mr. Waldo?"

"Well, I prefer a woman who keeps herself more cloaked in mystery, who lets a man imagine what is beyond his vision." Mr. Waldo half closed his eyes, and his voice was almost a whisper. Then his eyes popped wide again, and he shook his head back and forth several times. "Miss Bitterman, that is irrelevant. I need answers, and I need them now."

"I know. Read." Miss Bitterman went back to the papers. Suddenly she looked up to Mr. Waldo, eyes wide in amazement. "Could toe hair really grow long enough to braid?" she asked.

"Now how am I supposed to know?" he answered.

"Can you imagine?" she asked. "I wonder how toe hair does know to stop growing instead of just keeping on indefinitely, like the hair on your head."

"Miss Bitterman," Mr. Waldo said, a note of pleading in his voice.

"These last two make me sad," she finally said. "Chad wants to fit in, and Megan seems like she could stand a good laugh."

"Any clues?" Mr. Waldo said. "Anything that tells me who did this?"

"Nothing I can see," Miss Bitterman said, shaking her head.

"Well, I knew it was a long shot, but I figured it was worth a try."

"Maybe you'd better talk to the principal," Miss Bitterman said after a moment's hesitation. "Maybe she has an idea about this."

"No!" Mr. Waldo snapped. "She's at a conference and won't be back until tomorrow. I'm in charge here today, and by the time she gets back, this will be solved. It has to be," he said grimly.

"What are you going to do next?" Miss Bitterman asked.

Mr. Waldo thought and thought, the vein at his temple pulsing. "I guess I better take Bronco to the bathroom," he finally said.

Bronco sprinted back to the table.

"What's going down?" Marcus asked.

"Waldo's mad about something, he thinks we're criminals, someone uses semicolons, whatever they are, Mel is a tramp, and Miss Bitterman has a thing for toe hair," Bronco said, looking very confused.

The rest looked confused, too, except for Marcus, who smiled and flexed his feet on the table.

Chapter 8

Miss Bitterman opened the door to leave Mr. Waldo's office.

"This is ridiculous," Tess said with a snort. "I'm leaving."

"Just be patient a little longer," Miss Bitterman said. "Mr. Waldo will let you go soon. I'm sure of it. You won't be in any trouble if you just let him work this through."

The thought of getting into trouble seemed to settle Tess back into her seat.

Mr. Waldo came to the door of his office, arms crossed, a frown creasing his forehead. He had rearranged his hair so that it once again crossed his skull from side to side. Hanging out of his suit-coat pocket was a half-eaten roll of antacid tablets.

"You've missed a golden opportunity to confess and redeem yourself," he said, shaking his head in disgust. "You could have made this easy on yourself and your colleagues here in this room. But no. I will find out," he said firmly. "I will find out, and you will never, ever do this to me again. Miss Bitterman, come with me."

He marched through the room and out, Miss Bitterman behind him.

"Don't even think about leaving." His voice echoed back into the room.

"I'm out of here," Marcus said.

"You mean you'd leave me here all alone?" Mel asked, stroking his leg.

"You wouldn't exactly be alone," Bronco said with a snort.

"Marcus, don't leave me," Mel pouted. Marcus settled back into his seat.

"Will you massage my neck?" he asked.

"Of course I will," Mel said, and she made sure her short skirt hiked a little higher as she got up to stand behind Marcus. "Just lean back and relax," she said into his ear.

"Marcus, man, listen to me. She's poison," Bronco said.

Marcus had his eyes shut and didn't seem to hear.

"You know, perhaps Tess is right," Julian said. "What can Mr. Waldo do to us if we all simply leave? It isn't grounds for lowering our class rank or anything," he said with a look in Tess' direction.

"Ah, come on," Chad said from the other end of the table. "Don't leave now. Don't you want to know?"

"Know what?" Bronco asked.

"What Mr. Waldo is so upset about. What do you think it is?"

"If Mr. Waldo is right, one of us knows the answer," Tess said, surveying the room. "If one of you is responsible for my being here, I think you should simply stop playing childish games, confess right now, and end this."

"Yeah, Bronco, confess," Mel said.

"I didn't do it," Bronco screamed. "Wait a minute," he said in a calmer voice. "I threw a spitball in

English this morning. You want me to confess to that, I confess."

"How immature," Tess said haughtily.

"Shut up," Bronco snarled.

"Who do you think you are to tell me to shut up?" Tess huffed.

"Who do you think you are to call me immature?"

"Well, if you are entertained by spit, then I certainly can't consider you to be much above a first or second grade mentality," Tess said calmly. "Maybe kindergarten," she said after further thought.

"Look, you snot . . ." Bronco began.

"Back to bodily fluids again, are we?" Tess said.

"Someday you're going to need me, and you'll be sorry," Bronco said, stabbing his finger in Tess' direction.

"I doubt that," Tess said with a laugh.

"You wait," Bronco said. "Some dark night your car is going to break down on I-95, and I'm going to be driving by, and I'm just going to laugh and keep going." He smiled at the idea.

"And throw a spitball, I suppose," Tess said with a snort.

"No, better yet, I'll pull over in my nice warm car while you're out there in the rain and snow . . ."

"Both?" Tess asked.

Bronco refused to be interrupted. "And you'll come running up to my car, crying about how your car won't work and you have to get to the library before it closes or you'll fail or something stupid like that, and I'll let you just about get the door open to get in my car."

"How sweet," Tess said sourly.

"And then I'll drive off, peeling rubber in your face," Bronco finished triumphantly.

"You're sick," Tess said firmly.

"I'd rather be sick than stuck-up," Bronco said equally firmly.

"Do you think we're here because of Bronco's spitball?" Chad asked enthusiastically.

"No," Julian said thoughtfully. "If that were the case, then all the suspects would be in Bronco's class, and we're not."

"I should hope not," Tess said.

"So what do you think it is?" Chad asked again. "Let's everyone guess."

Groans greeted Chad's suggestion, but eventually Bronco took a guess. "Maybe someone slit his tires."

"Again," Mel said pointedly.

"Stop picking on me," Bronco said. "Everyone's picking on me, and I'm tired of it."

"Don't whine," Tess said.

"Next?" Chad said, interrupting yet another fight.

"Maybe someone got into his computer and changed grades," Tess suggested. "That's it! That's why our class ranks are wrong."

"Maybe there's an investigation into unfair treatment of minority students, and we're here to testify," Julian proposed.

"If you're being treated unfairly, how come you're third in the senior class, president of Honor Society, vice president of Latin Club, and student council representative?" Tess asked.

"Undeniable ability," Julian said smugly.

"Boring," Mel said as she continued to massage Marcus' neck. "I think that someone sent Mr. Waldo pictures of him having wild, kinky sex and threatened to put them up all over school, like in the bathrooms and in the faculty dining rooms and on the front windows so everyone could see them as soon as they got in the building."

"What a gas," Marcus said.

"You've got to be kidding," Julian said. "Mr. Waldo having wild, kinky sex?"

"Mr. Waldo having any kind of sex?" Bronco asked in wonderment. "No way."

"I think this is all a big mind game," Marcus said. "Like there's secret mirrors in here and psychiatrists are back there seeing if we kill each other or something."

"Killing's not what I had in mind," Mel said, running her hands through Marcus' hair.

"I think that there was a terroristic threat phoned in to Mr. Waldo during second period, and the phone company knows it came from inside the building, and someone threatened to blow up the building or burn it down or something," Chad said, sounding as if this were an entertaining possibility.

"Don't you think they would have evacuated the building?" Tess asked.

"Not if they thought they'd got the suspect," Chad said. "Yeah, a phone call. Anybody could make a phone call."

"Bronco . . ." Mel's tone was threatening.

"No way," Bronco said. "I don't even know the school's number."

"You could look it up in the phone book," Chad said happily.

"That's assuming he knows how to read," Tess said with a snort.

Before Bronco could launch another protest, Chad turned to Megan. "What do you think?" he asked the silent girl.

She ducked her head even further down and shrugged her shoulders.

"It's okay," Chad said gently. "You can tell us."

"Thank you," she said softly to Chad, looking up at him briefly.

41

What she was thanking Chad for, and whether or not she had a theory, was never answered.

Mr. Waldo came back into the room wheeling a cart on which was stacked seven boxes. He was smiling.

Chapter 9

"Did you bring us lunch?" Bronco asked hopefully.

"No," Mr. Waldo huffed. Then that weird smile crossed his face again. "Well, perhaps I have," he said. "We'll just have to see."

"Mr. Waldo, are you sure this is a good idea?" Miss Bitterman asked him softly, looking pleadingly at him.

"Yes, Miss Bitterman. It's a superlative idea. It's bound to hasten this investigation, and isn't that what we all want—a quick and equitable solution?"

"Yes, Mr. Waldo, but . . ."

"Miss Bitterman, help me unload the first box."

Shaking her head, Miss Bitterman went to the cart and grabbed one end of the top box, the side of which indicated it had once held a case of copying machine paper.

Mr. Waldo looked carefully at the top of the box. "Julian Thompson," he intoned, and he and Miss Bitterman lugged the box to the head of the table and placed it beside Julian.

"Thank you," Julian said somewhat dubiously.

"Get paper to make an inventory list," Mr. Waldo said to Miss Bitterman.

"Inventory?" Julian asked, his head cocked in puzzlement.

43

"The contents of your locker," Mr. Waldo said with a smug smile.

"You can't do that," Tess said, exploding out of her chair. "According to the Student Code of Conduct . . ."

"Page 47, Paragraph 3, the administration has the right to search student lockers if there is reasonable cause that evidence of wrongdoing will be uncovered," Mr. Waldo interrupted calmly. "Do not, Miss Eisman, presume to tell me what I can or cannot do."

"My father . . ." Tess began again.

"Will discover that you have been treated fairly according to the policies of the school and the school district," Mr. Waldo said, his calm face beginning to flush.

"But you do not have reasonable cause," Tess pursued.

"You cut your second period class or," Mr. Waldo glanced at Bronco, "you have a history of misbehavior. That's reasonable enough cause."

Tess sputtered, but she didn't launch another protest.

"This is just like *People's Court* on TV," Chad announced happily.

"I will ask you to verify the contents of this box so that you will not be able to later claim that any of your property is missing," Mr. Waldo said, seeming pleased with himself. With a flourish, he lifted the lid of Julian's box and began to unload it. He announced each item to Miss Bitterman, who wrote it down on the legal pad she was balancing.

"Number one. A large cassette player," Mr. Waldo intoned. "These are forbidden in the building, Mr. Thompson," he added to Julian.

"So arrest me," Julian muttered, a scowl on his face.

"Two. Four cassette tapes by Hammer."

"All right, my man," Marcus said.

"It's my duty to keep in touch with the scene," Julian said somewhat stiffly.

"Three. Six books on Norman England from the school library," Mr. Waldo continued. He flipped to the back of each book before placing it on the table in front of Julian. "All overdue," he noted.

"No wonder I couldn't find any sources for my World Civ paper," Tess hissed. "You have them all."

"To the early bird . . ." Julian said with a smile.

"Eat worms," Tess said in a deadly tone of voice.

Mr. Waldo seemed to be enjoying himself. "Four. Three notebooks containing class notes."

"Bloodworms," Tess whispered to Julian. "Long, slimy ones."

"Five. Catalogs from Georgetown University, University of Southern California, Princeton, and Boston College," Mr. Waldo continued.

Tess snickered. Julian merely smiled calmly.

"Six. One brown-bag lunch."

"Aren't you going to inventory it, too?" Julian asked politely.

Mr. Waldo looked confused, but he opened the bag and took out the contents one by one. "One peanut butter and jelly sandwich, a package of Tastykake cupcakes . . ."

"Chocolate," Julian added.

"Chocolate," Mr. Waldo amended. "A boxed container of juice, cranberry," he added quickly, "and a banana." Miss Bitterman was writing quickly.

That finished the contents of Julian's box.

"Sign this list," Mr. Waldo said, tearing off the top sheet of Miss Bitterman's pad.

"Certainly," Julian said, signing his name at the

45

bottom with a flourish. "Obviously my locker and my lunch all pass inspection. May I leave now?"

"No," Mr. Waldo said.

Julian deflated like a pricked balloon.

Mr. Waldo and Miss Bitterman went after the next box, lugging it to where Mel was sitting.

"Could we do this in private, Mr. Waldo?" Mel asked, her voice flirtatious.

"Certainly not," Mr. Waldo said, backing away.

"Number one. Three paperback novels. *Passionate Pulsations, Be Still My Throbbing Heart,* and *Thrust of the Sword.*" Mr. Waldo dropped the books on the table as if they were burning his fingers. Considering the cover art, perhaps they were.

Marcus reached over and took one of the books. When Mel saw his fingers trace the cleavage of the cover model, she grabbed the book back.

"Two. Two cassette tapes by the Sex Pistols," Mr. Waldo continued.

"You sure are consistent," Bronco said with a laugh.

"Three. A white blouse, a blue skirt, and a . . . um . . . undergarment," Mr. Waldo said, his face blushing scarlet as he held up a bra. He quickly dropped it on the table and put the paperback books on top of it.

"Why do you have clothes in your locker?" Marcus asked.

"This is invading my privacy," Mel said.

"Why not? You let everybody else invade it," Bronco said with a laugh.

"I bet I know," Tess said with a laugh.

"What?" Marcus asked.

"That's what Mel's mother saw her go off to school in today. But she wouldn't approve of the little number you're wearing now, right, Mel?"

Mel didn't answer, but she was actually blushing.

46

Mr. Waldo had been counting out objects while all of this was going on. "Four. Twenty-three beauty cosmetics of one form or another," he announced, pointing to the pile of blush, eye shadow, mascara, and assorted other containers.

Marcus stared at Mel's face in amazement, then rubbed one finger down her cheek, looking to see what came off. Mel jerked away from him.

"Five. One box of . . ." Mr. Waldo's voice dropped to a quiet muttering.

"What's that, Mr. Waldo?" Miss Bitterman asked.

"One box of condoms," he said more distinctly.

"They're not mine," Mel protested.

"They were in your locker," Mr. Waldo said.

"Someone put them in there as a joke," Mel said, tossing her head.

Bronco started to say something, but even he thought better of it.

Miss Bitterman had Mel sign the list.

"Next box," Mr. Waldo said hastily. This time they got a box whose lid wouldn't fit on it. Wheels protruded, and the box was placed in front of Marcus. He immediately began to caress the wheels, spinning them gently.

"Number one," Mr. Waldo began. "I can't imagine what earthly use it would be in a school building, but Mr. Duke's locker contained a skateboard."

"I like it near me," Marcus said simply.

"Number Two. Six copies of *Thrasher* magazine."

"That's it?" Miss Bitterman asked.

"What else do you need?" Marcus asked, signing the very short list.

"Tess Eisman," Mr. Waldo said, reading the name off the next box.

"I still believe this is unfair," Tess said.

"Number one," Mr. Waldo said firmly, reaching

47

into the box. "One library book on Norman England."

"You missed that one," Tess said to Julian.

"Number two. College catalogs from Georgetown University, University of Southern California, Princeton, and Boston University."

"You're following me," Julian said.

"I certainly am not," Tess said. "If anything, it's the other way around."

"How many accepted you?" Julian asked.

"Wouldn't you like to know?"

"Number three. Cliff Notes for the study of *One Day in the Life of Ivan Denisovich* and *Catcher in the Rye.*"

"So that's how you knew all the answers in English class," Julian said, smiling.

"I knew them already," Tess said. "I was just double-checking."

"Sure, Tess," Julian said.

"Number four. Five textbooks and six folders containing class notes."

Tess smiled smugly.

"Number five. A typed paper titled "Administrators Unfair to Honor Students," Mr. Waldo said, glaring at Tess.

"It was an article for the school paper," Tess said. "They rejected it, but freedom of speech still exists, doesn't it, Mr. Waldo?"

"We'll see about you," Mr. Waldo said with a wag of his finger.

Tess' hand was shaking as she signed the list.

Mr. Waldo needed no help with the next box, which he tossed to Bronco. Bronco caught it with a grin.

"Let the record indicate that Mr. Broncoman's locker was empty," Mr. Waldo said.

"Don't like lockers," Bronco announced. "They're for nerds."

Miss Bitterman looked confused, then gave Bronco a blank sheet of paper to sign. He did so.

Chad's box was next.

"Perhaps we had the wrong locker," Mr. Waldo said to Chad as he opened the box.

"Nope," Chad said cheerfully.

"Are you quite sure? Perhaps you'd like to look at the contents before you say that?" Mr. Waldo tilted the box so Chad could see into it.

"Mine," Chad said with conviction.

Mr. Waldo unloaded the box. "Seventeen copies of *Playboy,*" he said softly.

"Chad!" Bronco said with admiration. "You have January's issue? The one with the girl with . . ."

"Yep," Chad said. "That's one of my favorites, too, but I think Miss March . . ."

"Sign the list, please," Mr. Waldo interrupted.

"Nothing says I can't look," Chad said, signing the list.

Mr. Waldo was shaking his head as the final box was placed in front of Megan.

"Number one," he began, rushing a little. "Six textbooks and six notebooks."

Megan's books made an impressive pile.

"Number two. Four pieces of what seems to be piano music. Correct, Miss Massapalo?"

"Correct," Megan said very softly. "Mozart."

"One cassette tape, no indication of contents."

Megan nodded.

"That's all," Mr. Waldo said, but as he put the music beside Megan, something fell out from between the pages and clattered on the table.

"And what is this?" Mr. Waldo said, picking up a

key and examining it closely. "Just what are you doing with a key to the auditorium?" he asked Megan.

Every eye in the room locked on Megan.

Chapter 10

"Megan!" Mel said in surprise. "You bad girl!"

"Excuse me, but I'll take care of this," Mr. Waldo said sharply. "Megan, where did you get this key?"

Megan lowered her head and said nothing.

"I'm sure there's a good reason," Chad said to her gently.

"A good reason for a student to have a key to the auditorium?" Mr. Waldo asked.

"Yes," said Chad simply.

"Well, Megan?" Mr. Waldo stepped closer to the huddled girl and began tapping his foot rapidly.

"Mr. Waldo, maybe you should give Megan a chance to think for a minute," Miss Bitterman said nervously.

"It doesn't take time to think about the truth," Mr. Waldo said. "And that is what I want, for once."

"You think we've been lying to you, Mr. Waldo?" Bronco asked, outrage in his voice. "How dare you accuse us of that. We're the hope of the future. When you're old and senile, we'll be supporting you."

"Now there's a horrifying thought," Mr. Waldo snapped. "Stay out of this, Bronco. Megan? I'm waiting."

"It was loaned to me," Megan finally said.

"See?" Chad said happily. "I knew there was a good explanation."

"Who loaned you a school key?" Mr. Waldo asked, hovering even closer over Megan.

"I'd rather not say," Megan said. "The person did it in good faith, and I don't want to cause trouble."

"Well, you're the one in trouble until you tell me who gave you the key," Mr. Waldo said forcefully.

"Okay," Megan said.

"What do you mean, okay?"

"I'll accept the blame," she said.

"This is great," Chad said. "Just like in the movies where the heroine goes to jail rather than betray the man she loves."

"Thank you," Megan said to Chad, "but that's not exactly what this is."

Mr. Waldo was tapping his foot so fast that it made a constant drumming sound. "Why did you want the key?" he suddenly snapped, making Megan jump.

"I'd rather not say," Megan replied.

"Why not?" he asked.

"Because then you will probably know who loaned me the key," she said simply.

"Megan, I order you to answer my questions." That frantic look was once again in Mr. Waldo's eyes, and his voice was squeaking.

"Mr. Waldo, perhaps you're being a little harsh with Megan," Miss Bitterman bravely interrupted. "Maybe you should just go in your office and think this through for a few minutes."

Mr. Waldo whirled from Megan to Miss Bitterman.

"Besides, even if Megan does have a key to the auditorium, that doesn't mean that she had anything to do with the . . . other thing, does it?" Miss Bitterman spoke with slightly more confidence.

"What other thing?" Julian exploded.

"Isn't there some rule against having *Playboy* magazines in school? Shouldn't I be in trouble, too?" Chad asked hopefully.

"I know why Mel would want an auditorium key," Bronco said darkly.

"Why?" Marcus asked.

"Because she could have sex right up there on stage with a spotlight on."

"Bronco, how dare you say that?" Mel screamed, then ruined the effect by giggling. Everyone began yelling comments, protests, and suggestions except for Tess, who grabbed one of her textbooks and began to read.

Mr. Waldo stared around the room in amazement. Both eyebrows were twitching, and he grabbed his stomach. "I'll be in my office," he yelled over the swirl of voices. Miss Bitterman nodded and followed him off. "You have two minutes to get ready to tell me the whole truth," he said before slamming the office door, making Miss Bitterman dart in to avoid getting hit.

As soon as the door shut, all the noise immediately died.

"Thanks," Megan said softly.

"For what?" Marcus asked.

"For distracting Mr. Waldo," Megan said. "I really don't want to answer his questions."

"Then you don't have to," Chad said.

"Wrong," Tess said sharply. "Megan, if you did something that has me shut up in this room with these ... people, then you have a responsibility to tell Mr. Waldo and stop inconveniencing the rest of us."

"Cut us a break, Megan," Bronco said. "I *really* have to go to the bathroom."

"Isn't that a little selfish?" Mel asked sharply. "For

once can't you put someone else ahead of your own little needs?"

"Little?" Bronco shouted. "What are you calling little?"

"Wait, now," Julian said. "We need to look at this logically."

"The only logical answer is for Megan to go to Mr. Waldo and confess," Tess said. "I've wasted about enough of my time for her."

"How do you know that Megan is responsible?" Julian asked. "All we know is that she has a key. We still don't know what has Mr. Waldo so upset."

"Well obviously if you look at it *logically*," Tess said snidely, "the key must be important or else Mr. Waldo wouldn't have been so upset about it."

"But it could be two different issues," Julian persisted. "He's upset about the key because of school security, but it must be something else, something bigger, that made him grab all of us in the first place."

"Well maybe Megan used the key to do the big thing," Tess said calmly.

"In the auditorium?" Marcus asked, looking very confused.

"Megan, you can tell us," Bronco said as sweetly as he could. "Did you torch the auditorium?"

"No," Megan said.

"Shoot out the lights?" Bronco asked hopefully.

"No."

"Slash the seats?"

"No."

"Did you plan to meet someone special there?" Mel asked, joining in the questioning. "I understand how sometimes it's hard to find any privacy in this place, if you know what I mean."

"No," Megan said.

"You just wanted a quiet place to study," Julian suggested.

"No."

"Leave her alone," Chad said. "You're all as bad as Mr. Waldo. Why can't you just trust Megan?"

"Why don't you just grow up?" Tess asked.

"Stop," Megan said, speaking loudly enough to quiet the argument. "Just stop," she said softly again. "This is exactly why I have the key."

"Would you care to explain that?" Julian asked.

"If I do, will you leave me alone?" Megan said.

"Maybe," Julian replied.

"Yes," Chad said.

"I have the key because I can't stand a full day of all the noise and arguing and just always being around other people," Megan began, her head down, not meeting anyone's eyes. "The only thing that gets me through a day in this school is going into the auditorium and practicing on the grand piano in there. That's all I want to do, be a pianist and let my music talk for me, but my parents didn't have the money to send me to a music conservatory and even if they did they probably wouldn't let me go, so I have to finish school here and then I have a chance at a scholarship to Juilliard."

"See?" said Chad, looking toward Tess. "I knew there was an explanation.

"My music teacher knows how I feel, and he knew that I was ready to drop out of school if I couldn't find a place to breathe, so he loaned me his key. If I tell Mr. Waldo, he'll figure out which teacher gave me the key, and I can't handle getting him in trouble and not being able to play any more," Megan finished.

With that, Mr. Waldo's door was flung open.

"Ready to give me some answers?" he asked.

Chapter 11

"Megan," Tess began.

"Doesn't want to talk about it," Chad quickly interrupted.

"She has . . ." Bronco said.

"To have some more time to think. She forgets some of the details," Marcus said.

"Why are you helping her?" Mel asked, looking at Marcus. "Mr. Waldo, Megan . . ."

"Should not have to speak if she doesn't want to," Julian interrupted, jumping to his feet. "Isn't it true that if the laws of the land and the laws of conscience are in conflict, a person should follow the laws of conscience?"

"Where did you learn that?" Mr. Waldo asked in amazement.

"English class," Julian said.

"Who is your teacher? Who is teaching such radical behavior?" Mr. Waldo asked, quickly losing his composure.

"It's from Henry David Thoreau's 'Civil Disobedience,' " Julian said. "It's in our American Literature textbook."

"It's a classic," Tess said snidely. "Written, I believe, in 1846."

"Eighteen hundred forty-seven," Julian said.

"Enough," Mr. Waldo shouted. "You continually avoid giving me answers. I know what you're doing."

"If we're annoying you, why don't you just let us go?" Mel asked.

"No," Mr. Waldo said. "I'll get my answers. Miss Bitterman, give me paper."

Miss Bitterman scurried to her doorway to get the legal pad from her desk, then returned to hand the pad to Mr. Waldo.

"Last time I gave you too much leeway by asking you what you knew about today's events," Mr. Waldo said. "This time, I'm correcting that. You have two questions to answer, and you'd better give me answers this time. My patience is exhausted."

"When did you ever have any patience?" Bronco muttered.

"You will answer two questions," Mr. Waldo said.

"Man, this is worse than English class," Bronco protested. "Why don't you just stick bamboo shoots under our fingernails or something?"

"Don't give him any ideas," Marcus said in alarm.

"Question number one," Mr. Waldo continued. "Where were you second period today? Is that clear enough for you? Let me repeat: Where were you second period today?"

"Uh oh," Marcus said quietly.

"Question number two," Mr. Waldo continued. "What do you know about Megan's possession of a key? Wait," he said, holding up one hand, "let me be more specific. What do you know about Megan's possession of a key to the Conroy High School auditorium?"

"I don't like those questions. They're boring. Can I have some different ones?" Bronco asked.

"No," Mr. Waldo hissed. "No," he said, his voice

going up dramatically. "Those are the questions. Answer them. Answer them honestly."

Mr. Waldo began to walk around the table, handing each student a sheet of paper. "Watch the semicolons," he said to Julian.

"Semicolons are the mark of mature writing," Julian said, staring at Mr. Waldo.

"These are the answers to two simple questions, not legal briefs," he said as he handed the paper to Tess.

Tess refused to raise her eyes from the textbook she was reading. Mr. Waldo placed the paper in front of her.

"I really don't care about the difficulty you had styling your hair this morning," Mr. Waldo said to Mel, handing her the paper.

"You're just jealous because I have plenty," Mel said, looking fixedly at the top of his head.

"I am prejudiced against students who are uncooperative, not students who ride skateboards," he said to Marcus.

"Have you ever ridden one?" Marcus asked.

"No, I haven't," Mr. Waldo said.

"You should try it. Here. Mine's right here. Want me to teach you a few moves?"

"No thank you," Mr. Waldo said nervously, but he did tentatively touch the wheel of Marcus' skateboard and give it a weak spin.

"Megan, there is nothing in your record to indicate a precedent for problems from you. Let's end this right here."

Megan didn't even glance up.

"I must admit I'm surprised at you," Mr. Waldo said to Chad as he placed his paper in front of him.

"Great," Chad said with a smile.

Mr. Waldo tossed a sheet at Bronco without a word.

"Ah, come on, Mr. Waldo," Bronco said. "You said something to everyone else. I've been waiting to hear what you'd say to me."

"Mr. Broncoman," Mr. Waldo said, staring at Bronco as if he were appraising a side of beef, "I do not like you."

"I'm hurt," Bronco said. "I really am hurt."

"Miss Bitterman, please monitor them as they write, and bring me their papers as soon as they are finished," Mr. Waldo said, returning to his office and shutting the door firmly behind him.

Miss Bitterman looked at the students, none of whom were writing. "How about getting started?" she asked. "Just write something."

"What were the questions?" Bronco asked.

"Second period, Megan's key," Julian said.

"Oh yeah," Bronco said, and with a sigh began to write. Eventually the others also began, and Miss Bitterman went to perch on the end of her desk.

When they finished, she collected the seven sheets and took them to Mr. Waldo.

1. Second period today I left school and went to the University library. I know that students are not permitted to leave, but the circumstances were unusual; allow me to explain. First period, we were assigned a new research project in World Civ. I dashed to the library as soon as class was over in order to sign out some resources, only to find that Tess had already gotten all the best ones. I knew that if I waited until after school, she would get the University ones, too; after all, her car is faster than mine. Hence, I left school, went to the library, used a friend's

card to sign out all the best books, and returned to school. I simply could not bear to see any more of Tess' smug smiles. I know I broke school rules, but it was for a greater academic gain.

2. The source of Megan's key eludes my complete understanding; therefore, it is only fair that I refrain from commenting.

P. S. Please note that there are only two semicolons in this, and they are exceptionally well placed.

Julian Thompson

1. I left second period because this school's library is woefully inadequate. Despite signing out every book there on the Medicis, I did not feel that I had enough sources for a research paper that would live up to my high standards. I was on my way to the University library when some idiot driving way over the speed limit cut me off, forcing me to slam on my brakes. The brakes pulled to the right and I ended up stuck in the mud because the shoulder of the road was not properly paved. I plan to have my father look into that. By the time some helpful passers-by pushed me out, I never made it to the library, and, not wanting to sacrifice any more classes, I returned directly to school. By the way, you might be interested in knowing that the car that forced me off the road looked very much like the one driven by Julian Thompson.

2. The Medicis concern me; Megan's key does not.

Tess Eisman

1. Okay, I won't mention my hair, although I know someone who is an absolute magician and might actually be able to do something with yours. Okay, back to the questions. Second period I was in the girl's bathroom. I had just seen John Grant, fox of the senior class, walk down the hall with his arm around Ethel Toffelmeyer. Can you believe that? Like she has anything that I don't have double of. Anyway, I was upset and angry and hurt, as you can well imagine, since I thought that John was going to walk *me* to class. So I stayed in the bathroom. I didn't smoke in there, so don't even *try* to nail me for anything like that.

2. Don't you think I have more important things to worry about than Megan's key? Do you know who John Grant is? Do you think I should fight Ethel for him? What about Marcus? I know he's not a wrestler like John, but do you think he has boyfriend potential?

Mel Savage

1. I'm only telling you this because you said you're not prejudiced against skaters, and if you hold this against me, I'll know that you lied to me, man, and that is way uncool. I spent second period today measuring the railing that goes down the center of the stairway from the second floor to the first. See, it's split in the middle, but

the two sides are just about the right width for my wheels. I've been having fantasies about riding down that railing (soon as I calculate that the slope isn't too steep), and then right out the front door and across the parking lot and then I'd just keep on skating until I was out of sight. I'd do it on the last day of school my senior year. It would be the most righteous exit you've ever seen.

2. Be real, Mr. Waldo. How does a key match up to what I've been describing? I don't want to skate through the auditorium, so I don't care who can get in there.

Marcus Duke

1. I was in the nurse's office, because I use her bathroom. The regular ones aren't set up for wheelchairs. I got my shirt caught in the zipper of my pants. There were kids in the office. I didn't want to ask for help. She forgot I was in there. Eventually I solved the problem and left.

2. Please leave Megan alone. She is very sensitive and you are upsetting her.

Chad Rheingard

1. There is very little
   that makes me truly
   feel worthy of
   being alive
   I was where
   I find that joy
   that lets me live
   with all the rest.

2.

Megan Massapalo

1. I hate essay questions. I WAS IN ENGLISH CLASS SECOND PERIOD!!!!!! The teacher was making us read an essay called something like the Myth of Syphilis about some guy who rolls a rock to the top of the mountain and then it rolls down and he pushes it to the top again and it rolls down again and he does this for eternity, which is even longer than we've been in this room. JUST ASK MY TEACHER!!! I'm sure she remembers that I was in class because I told her this was the stupidest thing I'd ever heard. I mean why didn't this fool Syphilis just refuse to roll the rock and she said it was a decree from the gods and I told her what Syphilis should tell the gods and she almost threw me out of class for my language.

2. So Megan has a key. Big deal. You should learn to go with the flow or you're going to have a heart attack or a stroke or something.

Eddie Broncoman

P. S. It's okay if you don't like me. I don't like you either!

Chapter 12

"Okay, did anybody rat on Megan?" Chad asked as soon as Miss Bitterman had gone into Mr. Waldo's office with their papers. Chad looked around the table expectantly, a huge smile lighting up his face when nobody spoke. "That's great, that's absolutely great. I just knew that nobody would do it."

"Thank you," Megan said softly.

"I didn't because I thought someone else would," Mel said sulkily. "But if Mr. Waldo doesn't let us out soon, I may have to be the one."

"But nobody else did," Chad said. "Aren't you glad you stuck with us?"

Mel just stared at him and then turned away.

"What we need is some information," Julian said into the resulting silence.

"No kidding, Einstein," Tess snapped.

"I mean new information about why we're here," Julian said sharply.

"Imagine my surprise," Tess said. "I thought suddenly you had a pressing desire to get the latest update on the black hole creation of the universe theory, or maybe why the dinosaurs are extinct."

"A meteor hit them," Bronco said with total conviction. "Big meteor. Smashed them into bits."

"I think the theory is that the meteor stirred up

dust which changed the habitat," Tess said impatiently.

"Nope," Bronco said smugly. "Right on their heads. Brains everywhere. I saw it on television."

"You saw the dinosaurs become extinct on television?" Tess said, sniffing.

"Perhaps you two would like to continue this scientific discussion at a later date," Julian announced, "but right now we have a more pressing need. Information about Mr. Waldo, remember?"

"Maybe we could sneak into his office and look at the papers on his desk," Chad suggested.

"How?" Julian asked. "He's right in there."

"I'm sure I could find out anything we want to know if I could get out of this room," Mel said. "I have my sources everywhere."

"Sources of what? VD?" Bronco asked.

"But if we walk out, then we've defied Mr. Waldo and he really can get us in trouble," Chad said.

"So we get in trouble," Marcus said. "This is beat."

"Maybe one of us could sneak out," Julian suggested.

"Right," Tess said snidely. "With the mob of people in this room, one of us would certainly not be missed."

"Sometimes Mr. Waldo isn't too perceptive," Julian said.

"He's a jerk, but he's not stupid," Tess retorted.

"You want information? Want to talk to people?" Bronco bellowed.

"I do believe that's been the topic of conversation," Tess said.

"No problem," Bronco said.

"No problem?" Julian asked.

"No problem?" Tess repeated.

"No problem? I like your attitude," Chad said.

"If that man follows me, get him back," Bronco said.

"What do you mean?" Tess asked.

"You're so smart, you figure it out," Bronco said. Then he began to bellow. "Mr. Waldo! Mr. Waldo, if you don't want a flood out here, you'd better let me go to the bathroom. I've been telling you for hours I have to go, and I'm done waiting."

Mr. Waldo's door popped open and his unhappy face appeared. "Just wait . . ." he began.

"No more waiting," Bronco said, and he got up out of his seat.

"Now is not a good time . . ." Mr. Waldo said, the student papers grasped tightly in his hand.

"Fine," Bronco said. His hand moved toward the zipper of his jeans, and he walked to the corner closest to Mr. Waldo's office door.

"Come with me," Mr. Waldo said, alarm in his voice. "You may use the administrative bathroom down the hall, but I'm not letting you out of my sight."

"Isn't that a little kinky?" Bronco asked innocently.

"I mean I'll be right outside the door," Mr. Waldo said, flushing red.

Out walked Mr. Waldo, followed closely by Bronco. Miss Bitterman was standing inside Mr. Waldo's office, looking out the open door. The six remaining students glanced toward her, then looked at each other, eyes staring.

"We have to get him back," Julian hissed.

"How?" Tess hissed back. The others stared helplessly at Julian and Tess.

Several long seconds passed. Then Mel screamed. It was a scream that would have done any horror

66

movie victim proud. High pitched and long, it echoed dramatically. Everyone in the room jumped, and Miss Bitterman ran to Mel's side.

"What is it?" she asked. "What's wrong?"

"Air," Mel gasped. "I can't stand being closed up in a room for more than an hour. Then the walls close in, and I think I'm going to suffocate, and I get panic attacks. I have to get out of here."

"Oh, dear," Miss Bitterman said, flapping her arms like a frantic bird trying to lift off. "Just wait until Mr. Waldo gets back and I'll see if I can . . ."

Mel's second scream was, unbelievably, louder than the first.

"I'll get him. Just don't do that again," Miss Bitterman said, leaving the room at a run.

"Cool, Mel," Marcus said, patting her on the back. Mel continued to stare around the room, wild-eyed. Seconds later, Miss Bitterman raced back, followed by Mr. Waldo.

"What is it now?" he snapped.

Mel began to gasp. "Walls closing, closing, air, air," she panted.

"Oh, really now," Mr. Waldo began.

Mel's third scream made all those in the room cover their ears.

"Miss Bitterman, take her outside for some air," Mr. Waldo said as the echoes died away. "I need to get back to Mr. Broncoman."

With that, a new sound began. It almost seemed quiet in comparison to Mel's screams, but it was definitely the bell that signaled a fire alarm.

"Yes," Julian said, leaping to his feet. Several others applauded.

"Stay right here," Mr. Waldo said.

"And burn? That is definitely illegal," Tess said, heading for the door.

"Cancel it! Cancel the fire alarm!" Mr. Waldo screamed to Miss Bitterman. "Nobody can go out there."

"There's no way to cancel it," Miss Bitterman said. "It's automatic once it begins, and the signal goes to the fire department. We can't ignore it."

"Make everyone leave by the back doors," Mr. Waldo said, still screaming at Miss Bitterman.

"Teachers know to use the closest exit," Miss Bitterman said. By this point, cheering student voices could be heard as hundreds of students streamed out of the building, happy for a break from class.

"The roof, the roof," Mr. Waldo yelled to Miss Bitterman. "Come with me. Hurry."

The students stared at each other in amazement. They had some new information, but who could make any sense of it? They dashed out the door, right behind Mr. Waldo and Miss Bitterman. As they raced down the hallway, a door marked "Men" popped open, nearly hitting Mr. Waldo. Out came Bronco.

"See? I was right where I belonged," he shouted as Mr. Waldo dashed by.

Bronco met the others as they headed for the front door, joining the stream of humanity.

"How did you manage that?" Mel asked.

"I have my ways," he said. Then he looked around. "Where's Chad?" he asked.

"Oh my God, we forgot him," Marcus said. The group turned around and started back, fighting their way through the surge. They found him a hundred feet back, slowly maneuvering his electric wheelchair through the crowd, Megan at his side.

"There's a wheelchair ramp at this exit," he said cheerfully. The other six surrounded his chair as they all left the building.

Chapter 13

The part of the student body that exited the front of the building was massed on the sidewalk and being urged away from the doorways by harried teachers. Mel immediately began to stand on her tiptoes, searching for one of her sources. She hadn't found a suitable male subject, however, before a girl known by all the seniors simply as Gossip bounded over.

"Where have you guys been all morning?" Gossip demanded. "Everybody's talking about you." Mel smiled at that.

"Yeah, your name gets called over the intercom and you disappear forever. Pretty scary stuff," Gossip added, a grin on her face.

"What have you been hearing?" Julian demanded.

"What do you mean?" Gossip asked in amazement. "You've been with Waldo for hours and you don't even know why?"

"Right," Julian said. "Amazing but true."

"Well I heard that there was a dead body in the front hallway, and you're all murder suspects," she said with glee.

"Great," said Bronco. "All I need is to be blamed for that, too."

"I also heard that there was an orgy going on second period under the football bleachers, and you

69

were the ones they caught," Gossip said matter of factly but with a gleam in her eyes.

"That's more like it," Bronco said.

"In your dreams," Mel retorted.

"Do you have any *useful* information?" Tess asked, shaking her head in disgust.

"What, you don't like my information?" Gossip said.

"I don't like my name being associated with such stupidity," Tess announced.

"Well, excuse us for being in your presence," Bronco said. "We didn't pick you, either."

"You've been shut up together all morning and you haven't killed each other yet?" Gossip asked.

Suddenly Chad interrupted. "Look," he yelled, pointing.

Everyone turned to see what he meant.

"Up there," Chad said, his eyes riveted to the roof of the building.

"I don't believe it," Bronco said. "That's Mr. Waldo and Miss Bitterman. What are they doing?"

The figures could be made out at the front edge of the roof.

"There's writing up there," someone yelled while pointing at a strip of cement between the roof's edge and the second-story windows.

"Mr. Waldo is a . . ." Julian read in amazement.

"What's the last word?" Bronco yelled.

All of them shaded their eyes, squinting to see the end of the sentence.

"He's trying to cover it up," Marcus said. "That's why he's up there."

"What's he have?" Bronco asked.

Gossip dashed through the crowd of students to get a better angle, but quickly returned. By this point, other students in the vicinity were following the group's upward gaze. Moment by moment, the interest spread, as contagious as yawning. As person after person saw others looking up, they too had to check out the source of the stare.

"He's got a tablecloth or something," Julian said.

They stared in amazement. Mr. Waldo had one end of a large piece of fabric, and Miss Bitterman had the other end. Together they managed to hold the cloth so that it covered the last word spray-painted on the building.

By this point, every student—and teacher—in front of the building was staring upward. For a moment a hush fell; then everyone began chattering, laughing, and pointing.

The bell rang three times, signaling the end of the fire drill. Not a soul moved, not even the teachers. Silence fell again.

Faintly, from the roof, Mr. Waldo's voice drifted down. "Go back to class," he said.

Nobody moved an inch.

At that moment, though, an answer was provided. It was the wind that did it. A tiny gust drafted the cloth upward, blowing it so that it actually covered Mr. Waldo and Miss Bitterman. Before Mr. Waldo could get the cloth back down, the final word was revealed:

WEENIE

The statement spray-painted in large red letters on the front of Conroy High School said

MR. WALDO IS A WEENIE

The laughter was instantaneous. One boy laughed so hard that he fell to the ground and rolled around.

After a few seconds, several of his buddies joined him.

The only ones not laughing were Julian, Tess, Marcus, Bronco, Mel, Megan, and Chad. Their mouths were frozen in open gapes.

It was finally Julian who broke their silence. "We've been locked up all day because Mr. Waldo is a weenie?" he said in amazement.

"He thinks I would spray-paint that on the building?" Tess said in horror.

Bronco finally began to laugh, and his laugh was deep and raucous, coming from deep inside. "I always knew it," he said, gasping to find air to speak.

"You did this, didn't you?" Mel said to him.

"No way," Bronco said, "but I'd like to shake the hand of the person who did."

"You did so do it," Mel persisted. "It's just like your childish sense of humor."

"How many times do I have to tell you that I was in English class?" Bronco said, but his anger was drowned out in more laughter.

Teachers finally began herding students back into the building.

"I'm going to class," Tess announced. "There's no possible way that Mr. Waldo can suspect me of such infantile behavior."

"You're kidding," Chad said.

"What do you mean?" Tess asked.

"You'd miss seeing what Mr. Waldo does next?" Chad asked in amazement.

"Sorry, Chad, but I'd rather see John Grant than Mr. Waldo," Mel announced.

"Isn't that him walking back into the building with his arm around Ethel?" Bronco asked innocently.

Mel stared, a scowl slitting her eyes and wrinkling her forehead.

With no further discussion, the seven headed back into the building and returned to the room outside Mr. Waldo's office. They resumed their seats around the table. Neither Mr. Waldo nor Miss Bitterman had come back yet, and everyone's attention was fixed on the doorway.

"Isn't this great?" Chad asked enthusiastically. "We're right in the middle of the scandal."

"No wonder Mr. Waldo wanted to send you back to class," Mel said distractedly.

"Are you saying I couldn't have done it?" Chad asked, the normally cheerful tone leaving his voice. "I could have."

"How?" Mel asked.

"It would be hard, but I could do it," Chad insisted.

"Did you?" Tess asked.

"Maybe," Chad said.

"You got your wheelchair to the roof, leaned over, and spray-painted the building?" Tess asked.

"Maybe," Chad answered smugly.

"Cool," Marcus said.

"After all, who would ever suspect me?" Chad asked. "I have more opportunity than anybody else. I get away with murder around here."

"Murder?" Mel asked, remembering Gossip's rumor.

"Just a figure of speech," Chad said.

"Mr. Waldo is a weenie," Bronco said, shaking his head and smiling. "I like the sound of that."

"Alliteration," Tess said.

"What?" Bronco said.

"The repetition of an initial sound," Tess said, annoyed at his ignorance.

"Why don't you just skip the rest of high school

and go straight to being an English teacher?" Bronco asked her.

"Not enough money," Tess snapped back.

Footsteps sounded in the hallway.

Seven heads turned in unison.

"It's the weenie," Bronco whispered.

Chapter 14

To their disappointment, it wasn't Mr. Waldo. It was Miss Bitterman.

"Oh, my," she said as she entered the room, her red hair even more disheveled than usual. "Oh, my."

"Saw you up on the roof," Bronco said to her.

"Oh, my," she said again.

"Where is the weenie?" he asked casually.

"He's in the Main Office. . . . Now, Bronco, is that any way to talk about your assistant principal?" There was some anger in Miss Bitterman's voice.

"He'd better get used to it," Bronco said. "Somehow I think it's a nickname that will stick."

"Do you really think so? Oh, my, this isn't good," Miss Bitterman said.

"How about Mr. Weenie? Is that better?" Bronco asked innocently.

"May I have your attention, please? May I have your attention, please." Mr. Waldo himself was on the intercom, speaking to the entire student body. "This is Mr. Waldo, your assistant principal. If anyone has any information regarding the identity of the person who pulled the fire alarm, I need to know immediately. Also, if anyone has any information regarding the identity of the person who is responsible for the graffiti on the front of the building, please put the information in writing and drop it off at my office at the end of this class. All information will be confidential. Thank you for your cooperation in this matter."

"Smart move," Tess said sarcastically. "Now anyone who went out the back and didn't know about the graffiti will be frantically searching for someone who was out front."

"This is Mr. Waldo again," came the frantic voice through the intercom. "There will be a reward for information leading to the identification of the person responsible for the graffiti. A substantial reward," he said, his voice quivering.

"Can he do that?" Bronco asked. "Are there school funds to give rewards for people who rat on other people?"

"I demand to speak to the principal," Tess said. "This is not the way tax money should be spent."

"The principal's out of the building all day," Miss Bitterman said. "Maybe Mr. Waldo's using his own money."

"A little desperate, isn't he?" Mel asked.

"Beat scene," Marcus announced, shaking his head.

"Now isn't this better than a boring old school day?" Chad asked.

"Shut up, Chad," Tess snapped. "Can't you just once look at the dark side. This 'isn't everything great' routine is getting on my nerves."

"You don't have to yell at Chad," Mel said. "It's not his fault that your precious grade point average is at risk."

"She's right, Tess," Julian said smugly.

"How dare you?" Tess shouted at Julian. "How dare you say that? You're the one who ran me off the road on the way to the library, aren't you? You did it because you knew I'd get the books before you. It was you, wasn't it? Admit it, Julian. You ran me off the road."

"What kind of car do you drive?" Julian asked.

"A red '87 Firebird," Tess said.

"Oops," Julian said.

"Oops?" Tess shrieked. "You almost killed me and all you can say is oops?"

"Well, you were going awfully slow, and I was in a hurry," Julian said calmly.

"I was going the speed limit," Tess yelled, getting up out of her chair to tower over Julian, who was sitting calmly, a smile on his face. "You knew it was me, and you did it deliberately. Admit it, Julian. Admit it!"

"Prove it in a court of law," Julian said quietly.

"Hah! Got you on that one," Mel said, leaping into the fray.

"Stay out of this, sleaze," Tess yelled at her.

"Sleaze? You call me a sleaze?" Mel said, leaning back and sticking out her chest. "A little jealous, are you?"

"Jealous? Jealous?" Tess screamed. "Jealous of you with your painted-on face and your padded bra and your stupid little drooling boyfriends? I wouldn't be caught dead with any one of them."

"I don't wear a bra," Mel said snidely. "I don't need to, unlike some others in this room."

Miss Bitterman crossed her arms over her scrawny chest.

"At least I don't flaunt myself like some cheap tramp at every male that walks by," Tess hissed.

"When you don't have anything to flaunt, it's not much of a choice, is it, Tess?" Mel seemed to be enjoying the battle.

"Now, Mel," Marcus said after a moment. "Why don't you just chill out a little here and be nice to Tess?"

"Chill out, Marcus? Whose side are you on? She called me a sleaze."

"Truth hurts, doesn't it?" Bronco threw in.

"Shut up, Bronco," Mel said, now showing anger.

"You going to make me?" Bronco asked.

"Surely there's some way to resolve all of this," Chad said tentatively.

"Shut up, Chad," several voices said at once.

"Just trying to help," Chad said.

"There's no help for Mel," Bronco said, getting things stirred up again.

"Or for unethical jerks like Julian," Tess said.

"What do you call that—'jerk', 'Julian'?" Bronco asked.

"The truth," Tess announced.

"No," Bronco said. "That other word."

"Alliteration," Tess said.

"Waldo—weenie, Julian—jerk, big day for alliteration," Bronco said, pleased with himself.

"Look at Bronco, learned a new word," Mel snapped. "What's that make—three this year?"

"Stop it." The voice wasn't low, but it was compelling. "Stop it, stop it, stop it." The words weren't yelled but rather were chanted, almost prayed.

Everybody looked at Megan.

"Do you see why I hate school? Do you see why I have to go play my music to survive? This is so ugly," Megan said, her voice flat, almost emotionless. "I can't stand this. I have to go."

With that, Megan gathered up the books and music that Mr. Waldo had taken from her locker and ran out of the room.

The silence that followed her departure continued for long moments.

Finally Bronco couldn't stand the silence. "Guess she told us," he said.

Chapter 15

Megan didn't get very far; in fact, she must have run into Mr. Waldo as soon as she turned the first corner because he marched into the room maybe thirty seconds later, escorting Megan.

"I understand how these people could make you tense, Megan. Believe me, I understand that. I need for you to stay just a little longer until all the information is in," Mr. Waldo was saying to her. "I should be able to identify the person I want any time now."

Megan slumped back into her chair, eyes not meeting those of anyone else in the room.

"Miss Bitterman, the class period is about to end. Please station yourself at the entrance to the Main Office and take any information provided by students. Make sure that their names are on the information so that they may receive their rewards, if that is justified." He looked at the assembled students. "It will be," he said. "Money talks. It talks even louder than so-called loyalty."

"You think someone will tell you who painted the building just to get a few bucks?" Bronco asked.

"Yes indeed," Mr. Waldo said.

"You're wrong," Bronco said flatly.

"We'll see," Mr. Waldo said. "The odds are even

greater in my favor since you haven't been loose to intimidate potential witnesses."

"Who would I intimidate? I didn't do it," Bronco insisted.

"We'll see," Mr. Waldo said again, going in his office and closing his door.

"I don't like his attitude," Bronco announced. "I can't believe that he thinks his few bucks will buy information."

"I bet it will," Mel said.

"You really think so?" Tess asked.

"Sure," Mel said. "You almost turned in Megan for free when Mr. Weenie wanted to know where she got the key."

"That's different," Tess said.

"Why?" Bronco asked. "A rat's a rat."

"Let's just suppose," Julian interrupted, "that you knew that someone in this room was responsible for that graffiti. Would you turn that person in?"

"You mean I knew for sure?" Mel asked.

"For sure," Julian said.

"For me it depends on who it was," Tess said.

"What's that supposed to mean?" Julian asked.

"If it was you, I'd turn you in for no reward except the exquisite satisfaction."

"What if it was Bronco?" Julian asked.

"I'm telling you for the last time it wasn't me," Bronco yelled.

"But what if it were Bronco?" Julian persisted.

"I'd turn him in," Mel said, glaring at Bronco.

"Would you take the money?" Julian asked.

"Sure," Mel said.

"I always knew you were a prostitute," Bronco said.

"I'd use the money to throw a party to celebrate

you getting kicked out," Mel announced triumphantly.

"What if you knew that I did it?" Megan suddenly
asked. "Would you turn me in?"

"Of course we wouldn't," Chad said quickly.

"Did you do it?" Tess asked.

"What if I did?" Megan repeated.

"My daddy always told me to watch those quiet
ones," Bronco said, looking at Megan with a whole
new gleam in his eye.

"You've got guts," Marcus said. "It's righteous to
stand up for what you believe."

"Do you believe that Mr. Waldo is a weenie?" Mel
asked.

"Who doesn't?" Bronco said with a laugh.

"Well, do you, Megan?" Mel persisted.

"What does it matter?" Megan said softly. "I have
a key illegally, so I'm already in trouble."

"Megan, you know you didn't do it," Chad said to
her.

"How can you be so sure?" Mel said.

"I just know," Chad said firmly.

"Why? Do you know who did it?" Tess interro-
gated.

"I did it," Megan said. "There. Tell Mr. Waldo and
go on with your lives."

"What about your life?" Marcus asked.

"That doesn't matter to the rest of you a whole
lot," Megan said. "I'll deal with it."

"Are you sure?" Tess asked.

"Yes," Megan said softly.

Tess got up and headed for Mr. Waldo's door. Julian jumped from his seat to stop her.

"What do you think you're doing?"

"I'm going to tell Mr. Waldo what Megan just
said," Tess said, shaking his hand away.

"Don't you dare," Julian said.

"Why not?" Tess said. "You heard what she just said."

"She's confessing just to end this and get away from us, not because she really did it," Julian said.

"And since when did you learn to read minds?" Tess asked sharply.

"If you'd stop thinking about yourself for a minute and look at her, you'd know that, too," Julian said.

"That's rather ironic advice from someone who ran me off the road and nearly killed me," Tess said angrily.

"You didn't come close to dying," Julian said. "There was some mud at the edge of the road, not a thousand-foot cliff."

"What'd you do, plan this out in advance?"

"Sure, Tess," Julian said. "I went over and over it in my mind. As I race to get to the library, if I see Tess, I'll wait until this exact place, then cut her off so that her car will go off into the mud. Do you really think I'm that cold and calculating?"

"Yes," Tess said firmly.

"You only see what you already are," Julian said quietly.

Tess froze, no retort snapping from her.

"Ooooh," Marcus said quietly.

"I'll confess myself," Megan said, her face tensed as if she were in great pain.

Just as she rose out of her chair, Miss Bitterman returned with a handful of papers. Some were full sheets, neatly folded; others were jagged scraps ripped from spiral notebooks. She looked at the kids seated around the table.

"Just be patient a little bit longer," she said, a pleading tone in her voice. She tapped on Mr. Waldo's door and went in.

"Let it ride," Marcus said, looking at Megan.

Silence came, and it was a tense silence. Miss Bitterman's emergence from Mr. Waldo's office broke it. "If you don't need me, I'm going to lunch," she said to Mr. Waldo.

"Lunch!" Bronco yelled. He started out of his chair.

"Just a moment," Mr. Waldo said sharply, quickly appearing at the door of his office. "Where are you going?"

"Lunch!" Bronco repeated, as if no other words were necessary.

"That isn't possible," Mr. Waldo said.

"You may not deprive us of food," Tess said. "You have pushed your authority far enough as it is. My father . . ."

"I'll bring you lunch," Mr. Waldo said, cutting her off.

"I'll have a quarter pounder with cheese, large fries, and a chocolate milkshake," Bronco announced without hesitation.

"Same for me," Marcus said.

"Garden salad with peppercorn dressing, croutons, bacon bits, and oriental noodles, and a diet cola," Tess said firmly.

"Cheeseburger with no pickles, hash browns, apple pie, and a regular cola," Julian said. Mr. Waldo was looking from one to the other in amazement.

"Large french fries, nothing else," Mel said. "I have to watch my figure."

"Same as Julian's," Chad chimed in. "What do you want, Megan?"

"Nothing," she replied.

"This is not what I had in mind," Mr. Waldo announced. "Some of you had lunches in your lockers, and I thought perhaps a school platter for the others. . . ."

"Mr. Waldo, I'd say this is the least you could do for us," Tess said coldly.

"Tell me what you want again," Mr. Waldo said, sighing. Orders were repeated as he jotted them down on a piece of paper he pulled from his pocket.

"Hurry back," Bronco said as he left. "We don't want our food to get cold."

"Do not leave this room," Mr. Waldo said as he left.

"Sure," Julian said.

"I'm out of here," Mel announced ten seconds later.

"I have a better idea," Bronco announced.

"Right," Tess said.

"No. I do," Bronco insisted. "Let's read the rat reports."

"Speak English," Tess said sharply.

"Let's read those slips of paper the rats gave to Mr. Waldo," Bronco said, heading toward the assistant principal's door.

"They're undoubtedly in his office, and he locked the door behind him," Tess said, shaking her head.

"You smart people sure don't know much," Bronco said with a disgusted shake of his head.

Tess got up from her chair, walked briskly to Mr. Waldo's door and rattled the doorknob. "Locked," she announced firmly.

Bronco took out his wallet, got his driver's license out, wiggled it in the crack of the door above the lock for a few seconds, and then pulled open Mr. Waldo's door.

"Unlocked," he announced.

Chapter 16

Bronco marched into Mr. Waldo's office and, sure enough, the student notes were piled on his desk. Grabbing the stack, Bronco came back to the table, shutting the office door behind him.

"Look at this," he snorted. "There's a bunch of papers here. I didn't know there were so many rats in this school."

The others, except for Megan, gathered around Bronco, peering over his shoulders.

"Do you want me to be the lookout?" Chad asked.

"You've been watching too many movies," Bronco said with a laugh. "With traffic this time of day, we've got at least twenty minutes. Come over here."

Chad wheeled over to join the group.

"Rat Report Number One," Bronco proclaimed, reading the top paper. " 'Eddie Broncoman did it. I don't have any proof, but look at the odds. Most of the pranks in this building for the past four years have either been done by him, assisted by him, or at the very least he knew about it. Did you know that it was Bronco who set those fifty white mice loose in the cafeteria? Or that he's the one who ran girls' underwear up the flagpole? Or that he caught a queen bee and put in on the principal's car so that a whole swarm of bees covered it? So why wouldn't he have done this, too?'

" 'I don't want to sign my name to this, but you can put the reward money in Volume M of the *World Book Encyclopedia* tomorrow morning before homeroom and I'll pick it up. Thank you. Your secret friend.' "

"Secret friend?" Bronco snarled. "Secret friend? It won't be much of a secret when I get done with him. Even if I do have to go to the library tomorrow."

"Did you really do those things?" Chad asked in wonderment.

"Two out of three," Bronco admitted.

"Which two?" Chad asked.

Bronco looked at Mel. "I'm not talking," he said. "I only got caught for one, and a certain person in this room might turn me in for the other."

"Next letter," Julian said, reaching for it.

" 'Dear Mr. Waldo,' " Julian read out loud. " 'This is part of a nationwide advertising campaign for Oscar Meyer. Can't you see that it is a compliment? If you want to give me the money as a reward for peace of mind, feel free to. Michael Washburn.' "

"Wonder what Mr. Waldo thought of that one," Marcus said.

"Probably wants to believe it's true," Mel said.

"You know, that's another reason why it couldn't be me," Bronco suddenly announced. "Weenic is not a word that I use. If I was going to paint the building, Mr. Waldo would be worse than a weenie."

"Why don't you try telling him that?" Mel suggested.

"Third letter," Tess said, grabbing the next one off the stack. " 'Mr. Waldo. Obviously this is the work of someone truly immature, so that means it was a ninth grader. Since you don't know which one it was, suspend them all. That way we mature upperclassmen can enjoy school without the rug rats around, and everybody will be happy. Signed, the Conroy High Senior Class.' "

"Not a bad idea," Tess said, laying the letter aside.

"You were once a rug rat," Julian said.

"No, I wasn't," Tess said icily.

"Oh yeah, I forgot. You've been mature since you were about four," Julian said, laughing.

"Three," Tess said, not laughing.

"My turn," Marcus said, picking up a ripped piece of paper. " 'The butler did it with a candlestick in the parlor. Get a life, Mr. Waldo.' "

"Sure are a lot of smart asses in the world," Bronco said.

"Nice for you to have company, isn't it," Mel said.

"Let me read one," Chad said. Julian handed him the next note. " 'Dear Mr. Waldo. It must be one of those seven people you called down this morning, and out of those, I think Tess did it. She's mean,' " Chad read. " 'If I'm right, I want my reward in small, unmarked bills. Send it to Bill Witaker in Homeroom 306. P. S. Don't tell Tess I turned her in. She'll kill me with that stack of books she carries.' "

Julian laughed loudly, doubling over at the waist and pounding his fists on the table.

"I'm glad you've having so much fun," Tess announced. "Bill Witaker won't be laughing when I sue him for defamation of character."

"Lighten up, Tess," Marcus said. "If you sue every person who says something about you, you're going to spend the rest of your life in a courtroom."

"Is that so?" Tess snapped. "Well, I'd rather be in a courtroom than in here."

"Next," Mel said. "We only have twenty minutes."

She reached over Bronco's shoulder for the next note.
" 'Mr. Weenie. As I sat in my second period class, I looked out the window and saw four terrorists wearing camouflage and carrying Uzis scaling the front of the building. They saw me looking at them and threatened me with the Uzis so I didn't say anything. I think that the Communist takeover has begun. They're starting by undermining the schools. Call out the National Guard! Send in the helicopters!! Declare a National Emergency!!! And, of course, for our own safety, cancel school for the rest of the week!!!! At this very moment, poison gas may be coming in the air vents!!!!!' "

Chad sniffed loudly.

"Chill out, Chad," Marcus said with a laugh, picking up the next note.

" 'Bronco, Bronco
He's our man
If he didn't do it
No one can.
                    Love from the cheerleaders' "

Bronco smiled. "My cheerleaders," he said.

"They think you're a criminal," Tess reminded him.

"At least they know who I am," Bronco said.

" 'Dear Mr. Waldo,' " Julian read. " 'I would like to officially state that Eddie Broncoman was present for all of my second period English class today. I remember his contributions quite vividly. Perhaps there has been some misunderstanding that resulted in his inclusion in those absent from second period today. Eddie is no angel, but he does have flashes of perception that I try to encourage. Mrs. Calthern.' "

"The old bat came through for me," Bronco said. "I could kiss her."

"Perhaps you could settle for not calling her an old bat," Julian suggested.

"I wouldn't call her an old bat if I didn't like her," Bronco explained.

"Does that mean you like Mr. Waldo so you call him a weenie?" Mel asked sweetly, picking up the next note.

" 'Mr. Waldo. I did it. I confess. You'll never take me alive. Graffitiman.' "

"There!" Julian said. "Mr. Waldo has a confession. Now maybe he'll go after someone other than us."

"Right," Tess said. "Look up Graffitiman in the attendance lists. I'm sure it's there."

Julian shuffled through the notes that had already been read and put the one accusing Tess prominently on top of the pile. Tess snatched up the next note and read.

" 'Waldo. You think that's bad? You should see what it says about you on the bathroom walls.' "

"Maybe we'd better be a little nicer to Mr. Waldo," Chad suggested. "He's having a really bad day."

Mel began to read. " 'Mr. Waldo. Have you considered resigning as assistant principal? This job is obviously getting to you.' "

"I second the motion," Tess said.

Bronco grabbed the last sheet of paper and held it up. Scrawled in bright red marker were the words "Free the Conroy Seven."

"Not until after we eat," Marcus said, practicality surfacing.

"Mr. Waldo could be back soon," Chad said, looking toward the door. Bronco got up, used his license again to open Mr. Waldo's door, and returned the notes.

"Well, what do we know now?" Mel asked.

"Bronco did it with the butler who is really a communist ninth grader disguised as Tess," Julian summarized.

Chapter 17

Their timing was close; only a few minutes later Mr. Waldo rushed in carrying several large bags.

"Here," he said, taking out a hamburger and throwing it in front of Tess.

"That's not what I ordered," she sniffed.

"Where's my fries?" Bronco asked.

Mr. Waldo took out a container of fries and tossed it toward Bronco.

"This looks like a small order. I wanted a large order. Did you eat some in the car on the way back?"

"You ungrateful wretches!" Mr. Waldo screamed, throwing all the food up in the air so it fell out of the bags as it landed. "You sort it out. You're going to be the death of me yet." With that he stomped over to his office, unlocked the door, and went in, slamming the door so hard it rattled in its frame.

"Wonder if we'd get a day off from school for the funeral?" Bronco asked.

They quickly sorted out their orders and settled down to eat.

"How about some lunch music?" Julian asked. His cassette deck was on the table with his other belongings from his locker. He reached for a tape, too. "Hammer?" he asked.

"Oh, please," Tess said with a snort. "Don't make me listen to that."

"Fine. If you don't like my music, what would you suggest?" Julian asked.

"You can play my Sex Pistols tapes," Mel suggested.

"You want me to barf up my french fries?" Bronco said.

"You're disgusting," Mel retorted.

"Maybe we could play Megan's tape," Chad suggested.

"You won't like it," Megan said softly.

"Can't be worse than what else we have around here," Tess said.

"Is it okay?" Chad gently asked Megan. When she didn't reply, Marcus reached down the table and took the tape, passing it to Julian. He put it in.

Once the blank tape at the beginning hissed through, delicate piano music began. First the notes, soft and slow, were gentle, soothing. Gradually, very gradually, the piece built in intensity until finally, many minutes later, the last chords echoed away. All that could be heard was the silence in the room.

"What was that, Megan?" Marcus finally asked.

"Mozart," she replied.

"I hate that classical stuff, but that was okay," Bronco said in what for him was a quiet voice.

"Thank you," Megan replied.

"That was you playing, wasn't it?" Chad asked.

"Yes," Megan replied.

"What?" Julian asked in amazement. "You played that? I thought it was some professional."

"Thank you," Megan said again, quietly, not meeting anybody's eyes.

"No wonder you love to play," Tess said. "If I could play that well, I'd do it, too."

"If you love the music, then you practice to become skilled," Megan said. "The love has to come first."

"Yeah," Julian said. "Just think about how much you love good grades, Tess. That's how much Megan must love music, and more."

"More than I love skating," Marcus said. "Imagine."

"More than Mel loves sex," Bronco said, disrupting the mood. Everyone laughed except Mel.

A loud banging at the door that led to the hallway startled the group, and Julian clicked off the cassette player. Chad ran his wheelchair to the door and opened it.

"Sandman Sandblasters," a large man dressed in coveralls shouted. "You deface it, we erase it."

"Yes?" Chad asked.

"Is there a Mr. Waldo here? Ordered some rush-rush sandblasting? Said it couldn't wait until tomorrow no matter how busy we were?"

The door to Mr. Waldo's office crashed back against the wall. "I'm Mr. Waldo," he announced, striding rapidly over to the workman.

"Guess you don't like being called a weenie," the man boomed. "Can't say I blame you, but on the other hand, you got away lucky. Why just the other day, I had to blast a wall over at that high school across town. You wouldn't believe what it said. Called their principal . . ."

"Come with me," Mr. Waldo said, quickly ushering the man away. "Let me show you the easiest way up to the roof."

"We'll be right here waiting for you," Bronco yelled after him.

"Mr. Broncoman," Mr. Waldo yelled, but he

couldn't seem to finish the sentence, and the sand-blaster's loud voice echoed away as they left.

"Wonder what will happen to the person who did this," Julian mused.

"If Mr. Waldo ever figures it out," Mel said. "And that's a big if."

"I'd like to know," Megan said.

"So would I," Chad added.

"I know how to find out," Tess said calmly.

"How?" Julian asked, curiosity filling his voice.

"Ask my father," Tess replied.

"Oh, yes, the great lawyer," Julian said.

"So let's call him," Marcus suggested.

Everyone looked at Mr. Waldo's closed door.

"Bronco?" Julian finally suggested delicately.

"If I get caught at this, you're responsible, too," Bronco said, but there was pride in the way he pulled out his license with a flourish.

"Maybe we should try Miss Bitterman's office this time," Tess suggested.

"One card fits all," Bronco said, swaggering to that door.

"This time I am going to stand watch," Chad said nervously. "Miss Bitterman should be back from lunch any minute now." He took his position at the door, cracking it open so that he could peek out.

Bronco promptly opened the inner office door, and Tess leaned over the desk that Miss Bitterman had shoved partly back in but which still blocked entrance to the room. Tess grabbed the phone, pulling it closer, and quickly dialed.

"Yes, may I speak to Mr. Eisman please?" she said authoritatively. "This is his daughter."

There was a pause, and Tess impatiently drummed her nails on Miss Bitterman's desk.

"I don't care if he is in a meeting, tell him that his

daughter must speak to him immediately. It is urgent, do you understand?"

Julian smirked a little at Tess' difficulty, and Tess saw his look and whirled away from him.

"Daddy? I must have some information. Do you have that copy of my school's Code of Conduct that I got for you the last time I had a question about my rights?"

Julian snorted.

"Good," Tess said. "Now I need for you to tell me what the maximum penalty would be for spray-painting an insulting statement about an assistant principal on the front of the building."

There was a pause before Tess said, in a highly aggrieved tone, "Daddy! How could you even ask that of me? Of course I didn't do it. I need to know for a friend."

Another pause lengthened, and Julian looked toward Chad, who was intent at his post.

"No, I don't think it involved profanity," Tess said. "Unless you consider weenie to be a profanity. I think it's just immature, though."

"Bet that's the first time he's been asked to make a legal judgment on whether or not weenie is profanity," Bronco said with a laugh.

"Yes, Daddy. What is the worst that could be done? I guess we can assume that it is a first offense," she said, with a dubious look at Bronco.

Bronco shook his head, mouthing the words "not me."

"Are you sure?" Tess asked. "That's according to the Student Code of Conduct?"

"Bet he loves this," Julian said to the rest. "She calls him for advice and then doubts that he's right."

Tess wheeled to face him, holding up a finger to

shush him. "Thanks, Daddy," she said. "No, I'll call you if I need you."

"Well?" Bronco said as Tess hung up the phone and pulled Miss Bitterman's door closed again.

"According to school policy, the offender gets a five-day suspension, parent conference before returning to school, and may be required to make restitution."

"What's that mean here?" Bronco asked.

"I guess it would be to pay for the sandblasting," Julian said. "I can't think of any other expenses that this has caused."

"Maybe pay for a psychiatrist for Mr. Waldo," Mel suggested.

"He needed one before this," Bronco said with a laugh. "How much do you think sandblasting would cost?"

"How should I know?" Tess said. "That's not one of my normal expenses."

"How can we find out?" Bronco said. "I'm kind of curious now."

"Another phone call?" Mel suggested.

"My license is going to get worn out if I have to use it much more," Bronco said, but he was already heading for Miss Bitterman's door.

"Alert!" Chad yelled. "Alert! Seats! Places! Miss Bitterman's coming!"

"Real subtle," Bronco said. "Try not to yell next time."

Chad just got back to the table when Miss Bitterman entered the room.

Chapter 18

"Oh my, you're still here," Miss Bitterman said.

"Did you think Mr. Waldo was going to suddenly regain his sanity and let us go?" Bronco asked her.

"Perhaps," she said. "I thought he might realize that you're not bad kids, and cut you a break."

"Weenie Waldo cut us a break? Are you kidding?" Bronco asked in amazement. "When's the last time he ever believed a word a kid said?"

"Now, Bronco," Miss Bitterman protested nervously. "He just gets a bit overwrought at times. His poor stomach."

"*His* poor stomach?" Tess said vehemently. "You're worried about him? What about us? We've been held here all day without any proof. We're the ones being treated unfairly."

"Yes, but his health isn't what it should be, and really he isn't a bad man at all. It's just that . . ."

Miss Bitterman's words were disrupted by thudding footsteps in the hallway and giggling voices.

"Are you ready?"

"Are you sure you're going to do this?"

"I'll do it if you do it."

"All right. On the count of three. One. Two. Three." Silence, then more giggling.

"Come on. Do it this time. On the count of three. Do you promise?"

"Yes, just count."

"One. Two. Three. Free the Conroy Seven!"

Thudding footsteps and uproarious laughter followed the screamed statement.

"Oh, my," Miss Bitterman said. "This is starting to get a lot of attention, isn't it?"

"Well what did you think would happen?" Tess asked peevishly. "Mr. Waldo is defamed on the front of the building in letters five feet high, everybody sees it or hears about it because of the fire drill, and seven students, most of them innocent, are illegally detained."

"This is all getting out of hand," Miss Bitterman said. "Perhaps I can talk Mr. Waldo into letting you go back to class." She headed toward his office door.

"He's on the roof," Bronco told her.

"Now what is he doing on the roof?" she asked, alarm in her voice.

"Getting ready to jump," Bronco said.

"No! Oh, my goodness, I have to . . ." Miss Bitterman's flapping quickly gained the speed of a hummingbird's wings.

"Psyche," Bronco said quickly. "I was just fooling with you, Miss Bitterman."

"You're a bad boy sometimes, Eddie," Miss Bitterman said, her hands now clasped over her heart. "That was not funny at all. Not at all. Now where is Mr. Waldo?"

"On the roof," Julian said calmly.

Miss Bitterman wheeled on him, ready to start flapping again.

"Consulting with the sandblaster man," Julian quickly added.

"Oh," Miss Bitterman gasped. "Oh. Perhaps I'd better go help."

With that, she was out the door.

"Weird lady," Marcus commented. "Needs to chill out."

"Let's find out about sandblasting," Mel said, shifting the attention back to her direction.

Bronco leaned back in his chair, crossed his arms, and smiled.

"Bronco," Julian finally said. "How about opening Miss Bitterman's door?"

"I want to hear her ask," Bronco said, grinning, looking right at Mel.

"Forget it," Mel huffed.

"Come on," Tess snapped. "If we want information, we need to get it before Miss Bitterman gets back."

"Ask me," Bronco said.

"Open the door," Mel hissed.

"Ask me nicely," Bronco said, still leaning back and smiling.

"Open the door," Mel said in a near-civil tone of voice.

"Say please," Bronco said.

"I refuse to say please to an uncivilized creep," Mel shouted. "I'll do it myself."

She raked through her pocketbook, came up with her driver's license, and stomped over to Miss Bitterman's door, twitching her hips all the way. She put the license into the crack of the door, wiggled it, rammed it, and shoved it up and down to no avail. Finally she resorted to pounding her fists against the door.

"Well?" Bronco asked.

"Open the door, please," came Mel's muffled voice from where her face was leaning against the door.

"What was that?" Bronco asked.

"Open the door, please," Mel said more loudly.

"That was very nice, Melissa," Bronco said.

"Mel," she snapped.

"Melissa," he repeated. He went to the door, and she moved to the side, watching his every move. Within seconds the door was open.

"How did you do that?" she asked.

"It's all in the fingers," Bronco said smugly.

"Sandblasters," Tess reminded them in a bored tone of voice.

Mel found a phone book on Miss Bitterman's desk and turned to the yellow pages. "What was the name of that man's company?" she called back to the room.

"Sandman Sandblasters," Chad said triumphantly. "I remembered. I thought it might be important."

"Aren't you the happy detective?" Mel snapped.

"Good job," Megan said quietly. Chad beamed at her.

Mel rapidly punched out a series of numbers on the telephone. "Hello," she said, her voice low and formal. "This is the executive secretary at Conroy High School."

The rest of the students stared at each other in amazement.

"I believe one of your workmen is scheduled for a job at Conroy High School, correct?" Mel nodded at the response.

"Yes, the weenie statement," she confirmed. "These young people today simply have no respect for their elders."

Marcus had to cover his mouth to stifle his laughter.

"I believe that we failed to agree on a price for this service," Mel continued. "Could we clarify that now?"

There was a pause, and Mel looked back at the group calmly.

"Yes, I see. That strikes me as a tad high," she said. "Since we are a community asset and since we are, unfortunately, likely to have more business to send your way, might we have a discount on that?"

Again Mel waited calmly. "What a gas," Marcus said with a laugh. Even Tess had a trace of a smile on her face.

"Thank you very much. That price is much better. Please send the bill care of Mr. Waldo. Good-bye." With that, Mel hung up the phone and sauntered back across the room.

"Well?" Julian asked.

"Would you believe they wanted three hundred dollars?" Mel said.

"What did you get them down to?" Marcus asked.

"Two hundred and twenty-five," Mel said.

"Impressive," Marcus said.

"Why did you save this school money?" Tess asked.

"Didn't your father say that the person who did it may have to pay restitution?" Mel said.

"Yes," Tess said. Suddenly her body tensed. "Were you perhaps trying to save yourself some money, Mel?" she asked.

"No," Mel said calmly. "I was saving Bronco some money."

"Look," Bronco exploded. "How many times do I have to tell you? I didn't do it!"

"I'll confess," Megan said, quietly yet with a touch of desperation in her voice. "I already told you I would."

"But then you'll get suspended for five days," Chad said.

"So?" Megan replied quietly.

"And your parents will have to come in for a conference."

"They probably will anyway when Mr. Waldo punishes me for having the auditorium key," Megan said with resignation.

"And you'll have to pay two hundred and twenty-five dollars," Chad continued.

Megan had no response.

"It's better than three hundred," Mel said.

"But you didn't do it," Chad protested. "I know you didn't. And you said that your parents will only let you play the piano if you do well in school. What if they punish you?"

"It can't be much worse than this," Megan said.

"Oooh," Marcus said. "I guess she told us."

"Let's just end this. I'm in trouble anyway, so it really doesn't matter."

"But, Megan," Chad said, his voice rising unhappily.

"Don't you see?" Megan cried out. "I hate this place. All it does is keep me away from the piano. Every hour that I spend in class, every hour that I spend studying is an hour I'd rather spend practicing. I would be happy forever if I could just have a quiet room and a piano and never have to see this place again."

"No people?" Chad asked her.

"No," Megan said. "Just my music. Music never yells, never hurts. It's never ugly. It always makes its own kind of sense."

"So you'd pick Mozart over us," Julian said quietly.

"Yes," Megan said fervently, without hesitation. "Yes."

"And you'll confess to something you never did to get away from us?" Chad asked, confused.

"Yes," Megan said.

"Maybe she really did it, Chad," Mel interjected. "Maybe that's why she's so willing to confess. She just said she hates this place."

"Maybe I did do it," Megan said. "Maybe I didn't. It doesn't matter."

"Yes it does," Chad protested. "It does matter. This would go on your permanent record."

"When I play, my music stands for itself," Megan said. "It doesn't rest on what some pieces of paper in a school folder say."

"Well," Mel said. "I for one think we should take Megan up on her offer. It sure will end this mess."

"Isn't that a little selfish?" Bronco asked her.

"Who are you to call me selfish?" Mel snarled. "If you hadn't done so many other things to Mr. Waldo, maybe he'd be less uptight about this one."

"Okay fine," Bronco said. "I'll confess."

"What?" Julian and Tess asked in unison.

"Look," Bronco said. "Megan's probably never done anything wrong in her life. My folder, on the other hand, is huge. Mr. Waldo probably has to get help to lift it out of the filing cabinet."

Several laughs rang out.

"My parents have been here so often they're on a first-name basis with the entire administration. What's one more trip?"

"What about the suspension?" Tess asked him.

"Vacation time," Bronco said with a smile.

"What about the money?" Julian said.

"I'll find a way," Bronco said with less joy.

"Stop," Megan said. "I already said I'd confess."

"No," Bronco said. "I'll confess."

"I know," Chad suddenly shouted.

"No, Chad, don't tell me that you're going to confess, too," Mel said with a laugh.

"I have an idea," Chad said. "There's something we should do before we make this decision."

Chapter 19

"Okay, Chad, so what's your idea?" Bronco asked.

"Do you promise you won't laugh and that you'll seriously think about it?" Chad asked.

"Uh oh," Mel said. "This one must really be a doozy."

"Yes, Chad," Marcus said. "We'll be cool about it."

"What else do we have to do until Mr. Waldo gets back?" Tess added in a bored voice.

"Okay," Chad said, his voice filled with excitement, "here's the plan. Each person has to pick one other person in the room, and tell that person a secret."

"What?" Mel asked, laughing.

"You promised not to laugh," Chad said, biting his lip.

"You've been to a few too many boy scout camps," Julian said with a laugh.

"No, I'm serious," Chad said. "I learned about this at a conference I went to one time. It builds trust, and we sure could use a little more of that around here."

"Why should I trust any of these people?" Mel asked. "Besides, I don't have any secrets."

"That can't be true," Chad said. "Everybody has secrets. They're a healthy part of life. But if you can trust another person with one of them, especially if you don't know that person really well, then you have taken a risk that will help you grow as a person."

"Spare me," Tess said.

"Look," Chad said emphatically. "Do you care what these people think of you, Tess?"

"No," she said. "I couldn't care less what they think of me."

"So what's the risk?" Chad pursued. "If you tell someone in this room something personal about yourself, and you don't care what that person thinks after finding it out, then what's the risk?"

"It's not a risk," Tess said. "I simply don't want to do it."

"Afraid to let anyone see beneath that ice sculpture you've molded around yourself?" Julian asked Tess quietly.

"I beg your pardon," Tess snapped.

"Come on, Tess. Melt a little. There'll still be plenty of ice left," Julian said, some intensity creeping into his voice.

"Okay, Chad, I'll do it," Bronco said. "I'll tell the whole group a secret."

"This'll be good," Mel snorted.

"I sleep with a Mickey Mouse night-light on," Bronco said.

"You're kidding," Mel said with a laugh.

"Chill out," Marcus said. "Mickey is my man."

"Are you going to take it with you on your honeymoon?" Julian asked.

"Who'd ever be stupid enough to marry him?" Mel asked.

"Is this what you had in mind, Chad?" Bronco asked. "I tell everyone a deep dark secret, and they all make fun of me. Satisfied?"

"This isn't exactly what I had in mind," Chad said. "First of all, the secret should be a little . . . deeper and more personal."

"What's more personal than a guy's night-light?" Bronco asked, hurt in his voice.

"Second of all," Chad continued, "it is the responsibility of the listeners to be sensitive and understanding."

"You guys flunked sensitivity," Bronco said, crossing his arms defiantly.

"You're right," Julian said. "Bronco," he said in a solemn and deep voice, "I am touched and honored to have such special knowledge about you and your night-light. I now understand you better, and I feel closer to your spirit."

"I respect you, man, I respect you," Marcus added.

"Just don't let it go any further than this room," Bronco said. "I wouldn't want all the cheerleaders to know."

"I will never break the sacred trust," Julian intoned. "The words 'Mickey Mouse' will never cross my lips, even if I am tortured."

"Are you finished?" Chad asked, his voice almost angry. "Are you going to make a big joke out of this?"

"I think we already have," Julian said.

"So you won't do it?" Chad asked.

"We didn't say that," Julian said. "I'll do it if Tess will."

"Right," Tess said sarcastically. "I should trust someone who nearly ran me over?"

"You may choose any person in the room to tell your secret to," Chad said.

"I choose Tess," Julian said promptly.

"Okay, okay, I'm in on this," Mel said. "I choose Marcus," she said with a smile, reaching her arm out and looping it around Marcus' shoulders.

"I choose you, Chad," Megan said quietly.

"And I choose you, too," Chad said to Megan.

"I choose Mel," Marcus said, leaning closer to her.

"No fair," Bronco protested. "I want to tell my secret to Chad, and he's already taken."

"No problem," Chad said with a smile. "You just have to wait a few minutes." Chad's eyes were bright, and his smile didn't fade.

"Tess?" Chad asked.

"This is silly," Tess said sharply.

"Afraid?" Julian asked her.

"I choose Julian," Tess said firmly. "I am *not* afraid," she said, turning to face Julian directly.

"Good," he said.

"Great," Chad said. "This is absolutely great. Now we need to split up so that our conversations aren't overheard."

"I can't believe we're really doing this," Tess said. Then she got up, and pulling her chair with her, she moved to the corner closest to Mr. Waldo's office. "Get over here, Julian," she said. "Let's get this over with."

Julian took his chair and joined her. Marcus and Mel went to the far corner nearest the hallway, sitting on the floor facing into the corner, knees touching. Chad wheeled to the corner near Miss Bitterman's office, and Megan took a chair to join him there. Only Bronco was left sitting alone at the big table.

"Don't worry, Bronco," Chad called to him. "I'll be with you in a few minutes."

"Thank you," Bronco said politely, as if he were waiting for the doctor to see him.

"I can't believe nobody wants to tell *me* a secret," Bronco said petulantly, almost to himself. "And I told about Mickey."

Chapter 20

"You start," Mel said to Marcus.

"Why me?"

"Because I don't want to," Mel said simply.

"Okay," Marcus agreed.

Silence stretched. Marcus rubbed his forehead, shifted his legs, and settled more comfortably on the floor.

"Look, Marcus, we don't have to do this. We can just sit here and talk about nothing and tell Chad we shared secrets and nobody will know the difference."

"No," Marcus said. "I just don't know where to start. This is embarrassing."

"You don't need to be embarrassed. It only takes one look to know how cool you are," Mel said flirtatiously.

"Actually, that's part of it," Marcus said. "See this shirt?" He pointed to the front of his black T-shirt. The design on it prominently featured a Day-Glo skateboard. "The other skaters and I had these specially printed." He turned to show Mel the lettering on the back: Skate Posse Summer Tour of Love.

"All the guys and I do is talk about our summer tour," Marcus began. "We spend hours, days, fantasizing about all the ramps and tubes and tricks, how we'll be so great that we'll get a sponsor, free equipment, entry into the best competitions, travel all over the country, girls falling all over us at every stop because we're so obviously cool."

"So what's the secret?" Mel asked. "Everybody in school has heard about your plans."

"The secret is it's not going to happen," Marcus said. "It's all just a dream, just a part of an image we're trying to make for ourselves. Even down to the way we talk."

"You mean beat and cool and all that?" Mel asked.

"Do you realize that I have to actually remember to talk that way?" Marcus said. "It's because the rest of the guys do, and I wouldn't fit in with them if I didn't. It makes me like part of the club."

"So what's wrong with that?" Mel asked.

"It's not real," Marcus said. "Deep down inside there's a person who never would say cool, and who knows that this summer he's going to be working in his father's hardware store."

"Oh," Mel said, reaching a hand out to his knee.

"I think the other guys still think we can pull it off, but the truth of it is that we aren't good enough to get a big-time sponsor, and we don't have enough money between us to get further than the next state."

"But what if you really practiced?" Mel asked. "You can do anything if you really put your mind to it."

"That sounds great. 'You can be a brain surgeon, son, if that's what you want' " Marcus said wryly. "But skating is fun. It's not a life. It's not a future. I can't be thirty or forty or fifty riding around on a skateboard."

"Actually, it'd be pretty spectacular," Mel said with a laugh. "I can see you at fifty, hair in a long, gray ponytail, wearing a three-piece suit but skating down Wall Street to your big executive job."

"I'm afraid that my big executive job is more likely working at my dad's hardware store," Marcus said. "I think that's why I started this whole Skate Posse Summer Tour of Love idea. I am scared to death that my whole life is going to be spent weighing nails and mixing paint. Now don't get me wrong," he quickly added. "I love my dad, and I admire him for all the work he's done building up the store."

"But . . ." Mel said in the resulting silence.

"But when I skate I feel free and rebellious and . . . young," Marcus said. "And when I work at the store, I feel like I may as well just settle in, get married, have kids, buy a house with a white picket fence, and give up."

"You make all of that sound so terrible," Mel said.

"It's not terrible, I guess," Marcus said. "I just don't want to get trapped. I want to travel and explore and be irresponsible and ungrateful and all those other things my father accuses me of being. After that, who knows? Maybe I'll want to come home and settle down."

"Or maybe you'll skate off into the sunset," Mel suggested softly.

"Maybe," he said.

"Or maybe you'll be the funkiest hardware store employee your father has ever seen," Mel said.

"Maybe I could cruise the aisles on my board," Marcus said.

"You're sure you can't have your Summer Tour of Love?" Mel asked.

"It'll take a miracle," Marcus said. "That's why it was so important to me . . ." Marcus started to tell Mel that the reason he had cut class was to measure that stairwell railing, to see if he could at least make the exit of his dreams, even if he couldn't have the rest of it. He caught himself, though. "But that's another secret," he said. "Your turn."

"Why don't we just talk some more about yours?" Mel suggested.

"No way," Marcus said. "Wait, I'm forgetting. Beat scene, Mel. Chill out and let me dig your righteous secret." Both of them laughed at his self-mocking tone.

"Mine is a really secret secret," Mel said. "In fact, I've been trying to think of a less secret one, but this is the one that really counts."

"You can trust me," Marcus said. "After all, what I told you is important to me." Once again he had dropped the skater slang.

"I don't know how to tell you this," Mel said, and she completely broke eye contact, looking down at the floor, fooling with some of her bracelets.

"Just say it," Marcus said.

"Nobody at school knows this," Mel said.

"That's why it's a secret," Marcus said patiently.

"And I'd die if anybody found out," she continued.

"I won't tell anybody."

"Do you promise?"

"Yes, Mel, I promise."

There was a long pause, and then her words came out in a rush. "I'm a virgin."

Marcus laughed, and Mel looked up at him with a scowl.

"Sorry," Marcus said. "I didn't mean to laugh. It's just that you made it sound like you had something terrible to confess."

"It is terrible," Mel said.

"It is not," Marcus said. "It's fine."

"But it would ruin my reputation," Mel said.

"You're amazing," Marcus said, laughing again. "Most girls are afraid that they'll ruin their reputation if they lose their virginity, and you're afraid people will find out that you still have yours."

"If you asked anybody in this school, they'd tell you I've slept with half the boys here."

"How do those rumors get started?" Marcus asked.

"The girls spread them to make me look cheap, and the guys I go out with say that they slept with me because it would hurt their precious male egos to admit that I wouldn't do it with them since they're sure I did it with everybody else."

"So why don't you want people to know the truth?"

"My reputation gets me lots of attention and lots of dates," Mel said simply.

"You could get plenty of both without having a sleazy reputation," Marcus said somewhat undiplomatically.

"Oh could I?" Mel asked. "Let me tell you. In ninth and tenth grade I looked like exactly what I was—a good little Catholic girl who went to confession every week even though she had to make up sins to confess and who went to mass every Sunday and who had a holy medal pinned to her bra."

Marcus chuckled again, then stifled it. "Sorry," he said. "I was just picturing you."

"That's about what everyone else did," Mel said. "They laughed at me or ignored me because I was this prim girl with these high-necked dresses who gasped in horror if someone cursed."

"So what happened?" Marcus asked.

"Nothing, and everything," Mel said. "Nothing, because inside I'm still a good girl. Everything, because the summer before eleventh grade, I decided that I was sick of being ignored. I bought a few new outfits, lots of makeup and jewelry, and changed from sweet little Melissa into Mel the sex kitten."

"The sex kitten who doesn't put out," Marcus said.

"Right," Mel said.

"What happened at school?" Marcus asked.

"Everything," Mel said. "I had boys tripping over each other to ask me out, the same ones who had looked right through me the year before. I actually had guys I'd gone to school with since first grade ask me if I'd just transferred in this year. You wouldn't believe how a short skirt, high heels, a tight top, and a bad reputation help your social life around here."

"But that's not fair," Marcus protested.

"Tell me about it," Mel said. "It may not be fair, but it's the only game in town."

"You mean you don't mind having people think you're something you're not?"

"Sure I mind," Mel said seriously. "But I've come to realize that I really do love attention, and this is the only way I know how to get it."

"There are lots of guys who would like you for the person you really are," Marcus said.

"Name one," Mel snapped back.

"You act like high school boys only have one thing on their minds," Marcus protested.

"They do," Mel said immediately.

"You're right," Marcus replied with a laugh. "But once we get past that, we actually do care about the real person."

"If a guy won't give you a chance unless you look promising, then your theory doesn't work too well, does it?"

"What about all the guys you date? What happens when they realize that you're not the kind of girl they thought you were?"

"A few ask me out again. Most don't."

"God, you make me ashamed to be male," Marcus said.

"Don't take God's name in vain," Mel said with a small laugh.

"High school really is a screwed-up scene," Marcus said with a shake of his head.

"But what's our option—the real world?" Mel asked.

"Skate Posse Summer Tour of Love," Marcus said sadly.

"Hey, baby," Mel said with a sexy smile, leaning forward to him and kissing him right on the lips.

Somehow, though, it wasn't a sexual kiss. It was friendly, almost chaste. Marcus reached out and hugged her, and his hands stayed firmly on the center of her back, not roving an inch.

Chapter 21

"Are we really going to do this?" Tess asked Julian with a sigh.

"Yes," Julian replied.

"Why?"

"Because we promised Chad we would, for starters. Also, I don't think it will kill us to tell one secret. I'm sure we'll both have plenty left."

"Okay," Tess said in a bored voice. "You start."

"Why me? You start."

"Why must you make this so difficult? I don't want to do it in the first place."

"Fine," Julian said. "I'll start." He gazed away from Tess, deep in thought. When he finally spoke, his voice was quiet and deep. "I think the secret that bothers me the most," he said, "is that I'm always afraid that I'm not good enough."

"What do you mean?" Tess asked in amazement. "You're always right up there with me when it comes to grades."

"I think I'm good enough for me," Julian said slowly. "It's just that I'm not sure I'm good enough for all the rest."

"Who are all the rest?" Tess asked, curiosity tingeing her voice.

"I don't just want to get good grades," Julian said.

"I want to be a leader. I want to be a role model for the next black kid who comes along and wants to excel. I don't want to do well just for myself. I want to do well for my race."

"That's a pretty big responsibility to set for yourself," Tess said.

"That's why I'm scared a lot of the time," Julian said. "You know how a lot of people think that black kids should be slam-dunking basketballs? I want them to think that black kids should be getting A's in physics and being a class officer and earning the respect of their teachers and classmates."

"You've done all that," Tess said simply.

"Have I?" Julian asked her, his voice intense. "Have I done enough? Have my four years in high school broken down any prejudices, made anything easier for the next kids coming through?"

"If it's any consolation," Tess said after quiet thought, "I don't think of you as black. I just think of you as my competition."

"I don't know whether to thank you or not," Julian said with a wry chuckle. "But it's not just school that worries me. It's all the rest. I feel like my whole life has to be perfect. I feel like I can't do anything wrong at all, can't make any mistakes, or I'll fail as a role model, or it will come back to haunt me later."

"But you *are* human," Tess said.

"I'm afraid to be sometimes," Julian said. "Sometimes I want to go out and get drunk, or have meaningless sex with the first girl I can get into bed, or refuse to study or do homework and get F's for a while. I'm afraid that side of me will win out one of these days."

"It hasn't yet," Tess said reassuringly.

"That's what you think," Julian said with a smile.

"You mean you have done those things?" Tess asked.

"I'm just teasing," Julian said. "I've only done them in my brain—so far."

"I don't think you have too much to worry about," Tess said. "It seems to me that deep down you're a good person."

"Am I?" Julian said. "I ran you off the road. Do you know how that makes me feel? Am I so absorbed with grades that I'm losing the rest of me?"

"You said it was an accident," Tess reminded him.

"It was," Julian said, "but that doesn't change the fact that you could have been hurt."

"I'm fine," Tess said.

"You know," Julian said, "I never would have believed that I'd say this, but I'm glad."

"See there?" Tess said. "You are a good person. Just remember to be humble and charitable when I get the top grade on that research paper."

"How are you going to do that when I have all the best books?" Julian asked smugly.

"You could prove your goodness by sharing them with me," Tess suggested.

"In your dreams," Julian said with a laugh. "Your turn. I want to hear your secret."

"No," Tess said.

"That's no fair," Julian protested.

"I never claimed to be a good person," Tess said. "I can do whatever I want."

"I'll tell Chad on you," Julian said.

"No, not Chad," Tess said in mock horror. "He probably has some worse game for people to play who refuse to cooperate. Okay."

"That's better," Julian said, leaning back and crossing his arms.

"I sleep with my teddy bear. There. I'm finished."

"Tess, that doesn't count."

"And why not?"

"I tell you that I'm afraid to let down an entire race of future leaders and you tell me you sleep with your teddy bear? That's not fair."

"Okay," Tess said with a deep sigh. "You know that my father is a lawyer."

"Who doesn't know that?"

"Did you also know that I have a sister four years older than me?"

"No," Julian said.

"Well, not many people do. She started out in ninth grade taking all college preparatory classes, decided not to work very hard and failed a few, got switched to general classes, and barely graduated with her class." Tess paused.

"So?" Julian prodded.

"So my father acts like she doesn't exist," Tess said, a note of disbelief in her voice. "My sister got a job as a beautician right out of school, and she's doing really well, moved up to manager. But as soon as my father saw that she wasn't going to go to college or anything, he encouraged her to move out into her own apartment, and he never mentions her. I mean he speaks to her when she comes home to visit, but he never acts very interested, never asks about her job or her friends or anything."

"That's a shame," Julian said.

"I know," Tess said. "I mean, I'm not really close to her, either, but she's beautiful and she's happy. She's doing what she wants to do with her life. It's not what I would want to do, heaven knows, but it's her life."

"Your father doesn't see it that way, though," Julian stated.

"No. What really bothers me, though, is that I

120

think my father would do the same thing to me. I mean, he is absolutely convinced that I'm going to graduate at the top of my class, go to a good college and then straight on to law school."

"Isn't that what you want to do?" Julian asked.

"Sure," Tess said, but with a touch of hesitation. "That's what I'm going to do, but what if something goes wrong? Will my father just turn off his love?"

"I don't see how he could do that," Julian said.

"I've seen him do it," Tess said forcefully. "I used to always believe that my sister was his pet, his favorite. I think she was until she started to do poorly in school. Then I became his shining hope."

"What about your mother?" Julian asked.

"My parents were divorced when I was in elementary school," Tess said. "My father used all his legal connections to get custody. I only see my mother a few times a year. She just says she wants me to be happy."

"Will being a lawyer make you happy?" Julian asked.

"Yes," Tess said. Then, with more conviction. "Yes. It will give me everything I want—money, power, prestige, a chance to prove myself and advance."

"And it will earn you your father's love," Julian said.

"Yes," Tess said simply.

"It's a shame that love has to be earned," Julian said.

"That's the way it goes," Tess said. "I can do it."

"I'm sure you can," Julian said, "but what will your father say if you finish second in your class or even third?"

"I don't want to think about it," Tess said. "Who could possibly be ranked ahead of us?"

"I don't know, but I'm sure you'll find out," Julian said with a smile.

"You're right about that," Tess said, the sadness slowly leaving her face to be replaced by solid determination. "Strange game Chad has us playing," she said. "I never meant to tell you all of this."

"Whoever said that your high school years are the best of your life?" Julian asked with a laugh. "It sounds like the two of us are prime candidates for an early ulcer or a lunatic asylum."

"It's got to get better," Tess said.

"It will," Julian said, but there was a strong dose of doubt in his voice.

"Besides, if you go crazy, that will make it easier for me to get the best grades."

"She's back," Julian announced with a shake of his head, "the Tess we all know and . . . tolerate."

Chapter 22

Chad and Megan, off by themselves, settled in to talk. Chad looked toward Bronco, sitting sulkily by himself.

"Megan, you can say no, but would you mind terribly if I asked Bronco to hear our secrets? I don't like to leave him there alone. I don't want him to feel left out."

"I don't mind," Megan said. "My secret is short and will only take a second to tell, and he's welcome to hear it."

"Bronco!" Chad called. "Come join us."

Bronco's face lit up, but then he made a point of slowly, nonchalantly strolling over, dragging a chair with him. "You told your secrets that fast?" he asked.

"No," Chad said. "We wanted you to hear them, too, if that's okay. Do you mind telling your secret to both of us?"

"I guess not," Bronco said. "It's pretty embarrassing, but I don't think you two are likely to go blabbing."

"Don't worry," Chad said. "After all, this was my idea. I'm not about to wreck it."

"Why don't you go first?" Megan said, meeting Bronco's eyes for the first time.

123

"No," Bronco said hastily. "I'm not ready yet. You start, Chad."

"Okay," Chad said. "I need to go back a ways before I can get to the secret part. I don't talk much about what put me in this chair, but I have to start there. Up until five years ago, I was a perfectly healthy, active kid," Chad said quietly. "In fact, I was a good soccer player, made the best team for my age division and everything. Then, during the summer when I was fourteen, my parents took my sisters and me to the beach." Chad paused, seeming to drift further and further away as he told his story.

"That's nice," Bronco finally said, sensing a need to bring Chad back to his story.

"It should have been," Chad said. "I was riding the waves, having a great time. I was a strong swimmer, and I'd been riding the waves every summer since I was seven. My father was right there on the beach with my sisters, watching me, cheering me on. Then a wave came a little stronger than the ones before but still not really that big. I didn't hit it quite right, and I got tossed around, just like I had hundreds of times before. Only this time, I got thrown down head first at just the wrong angle, and I ended up with a severe spinal injury."

"Oh my God," Megan said quietly.

"I guess I was lucky not to drown," Chad said. "My father saw that I didn't come up, and he came right after me. Otherwise I never would have made it out of the water."

"So one second you were a healthy, happy kid . . ." Bronco said, almost in a whisper.

"And in the next second, I was a quadriplegic," Chad finished for him. "Actually, I'm lucky to have some use of my arms. It took years of rehabilitation to get this far, and the doctors are amazed that I've regained enough control to draw, even though it is slow and I have to wear a brace."

"Will you ever walk again?" Megan asked. "I mean if you keep working, can you continue to regain more use of your body?"

"No," Chad said bluntly. "This is more than the doctors hoped for. They don't expect anything more."

"All from playing in the ocean," Bronco said in wonderment.

"Right," Chad said. "I mean if I'd been drunk and gotten in a car crash or dived into a shallow pool or done something foolhardy I might be able to accept this a little better. But all I was doing was something I'd done for years, something my dad was watching me do."

"It seems like you have accepted it even under these circumstances," Megan said.

"That's the secret," Chad said. "I haven't. All this cheerfulness and enthusiasm is an act—a good one, but still an act."

"What do you mean?" Bronco said. "Even when everyone was giving you a hard time, you still were happy."

"I still seemed happy," Chad replied. "Underneath, I am full of anger and resentment, so much that it scares me. Sometimes I feel like running down people with my wheelchair, screaming at people who take their legs for granted. But I figured out pretty early that it would be hard enough to gain acceptance in a wheelchair, and it would be impossible if I let people see the anger and depression."

"So you hide it," Megan said.

"Sure do," Chad said. "And you know, sometimes it actually helps. Sometimes if I fake being happy long enough, a little real happiness actually does seep in."

"But what about all those other feelings?" Megan asked. "Do they just go away?"

"No," Chad said quietly. "You'd be amazed at some of the things I write, and most of the things I draw. I scream at my mother, threaten to run over my sisters, and go through a lot of dishes."

"Dishes?" Bronco asked.

"My mother said we really couldn't afford a psychiatrist for me, so she goes to yard sales and buys every really cheap dish she can find. Then she set aside a part of our basement for me. Whenever I start to get crazy, I go down there and heave those dishes at the cement wall. My mom and I have a code. A bad day at school is usually a ten-dish day, a day when I can't get one of my drawings to turn out the way I want it to because my hands aren't very steady might be a fifteen-dish day, and a fight with one of my sisters is usually worth three or four."

"What's today going to be?" Bronco asked with a smile. "Thirty? Forty?"

"Actually, today has been such a break in the routine that I might not have to throw any," Chad said.

"Well, at least it's been good for something," Bronco said.

"Your turn," Chad said to Bronco. "That's enough about my dark side."

"My secret's stupid in comparison," Bronco said. "I don't want to tell it now."

"Come on," Chad said. "Be glad you don't have one like mine. Just tell it."

"Do you both promise not to laugh at me?" Bronco said.

"We promise," Megan and Chad chorused.

"It's about Mel," Bronco said, his face blushing red.

"What about her?" Chad asked, lowering his voice

as he glanced toward the corner where Mel and Marcus were huddled, engrossed in their own conversation.

When Bronco still didn't say anything, Megan tried to help him. "You hate her, right?"

"No," Bronco said miserably. "I wish I did."

"Bronco, come on. We promised not to laugh," Chad said firmly.

"I want to go out with her more than anything in the world," Bronco finally blurted. "I say terrible things to her and about her but that's because I'm afraid to tell her how much I like her and how much I want to go out with her. I mean, I know what all the guys say and about her reputation and all and that's not why I want to go out with her. She just has something that makes me have trouble breathing when I see her, and I think she's beautiful and sexy and smart and I want to take her out so bad that it hurts." It didn't seem like Bronco took even one breath during all of that.

"So why don't you ask her out?" Chad asked simply.

"I did once and she ended up going to the prom with someone else," Bronco said miserably.

"A prom might be a big first date," Chad said. "Why not start with something simpler, like a movie?"

"You see the way she treats me? She hates my guts. If I asked her out, she'd make a joke out of me all over school. And then if some smart guy ranked on me about it, I'd probably have to kill him, and I already want to kill every guy she goes out with, and if I kill all them, there aren't going to be many guys left in this entire school."

Megan's eyes had tears in them, but she managed to keep a straight face and not laugh.

"So what are you going to do about this?" Chad asked.

"Nothing," Bronco said. "I'm just going to suffer. End of discussion."

"I really think you should give her a chance. What do you have to lose?" Megan tried.

"My reputation," Bronco said promptly. "I wouldn't want the cheerleaders to know that someone would actually turn me down, even though I'd trade them all in for one date with Mel. Isn't that sad?"

"I think it's touching," Chad said.

"I don't want to be touching, unless it's Mel," Bronco said in a grumpy whine.

"Megan?" Chad said, looking to her. "Your turn."

"Mine's simple," Megan said, a touch of a smile crossing her face.

"So tell us," Chad insisted.

"I have a 4.0," Megan said flatly.

It took a moment for the full significance of Megan's revelation to sink in.

"A 4.0 for all four years?" Chad asked. "Straight A's?"

Megan nodded.

"So you're the one who's ranked above Tess and Julian," Chad said with a smile.

Megan nodded again.

"Way to go," Bronco said, clapping Megan on the back. "They're fighting and clawing and you just glide right by and outdo them both."

"It's kind of funny," Megan said. "I have what they want, and I really don't care about it at all."

"You don't care that you have straight A's?" Chad asked.

"No," Megan said simply. "For me, it was just insurance that my parents would let me keep playing the piano. They always said that if my grades slipped at all, they'd stop my lessons. I didn't want to give them any excuse."

"Why don't Tess and Julian know about you?" Chad asked.

"Because I don't talk about it," Megan said. "I do all the work, but I don't participate much in class or discuss grades. Tess and Julian fight it out for the top score, and I settle for the low A's."

"You will be valedictorian of the senior class, and you don't even like this school," Bronco said.

"I hate it," Megan said simply.

"That should be some graduation speech," Chad said with a low whistle.

"It just might be," Megan said. "Actually, I often think it would be much easier if I just got one B. It would make Tess and Julian happy, and it would simplify things for me. I don't think my parents would be too unhappy with just one B."

"My parents would be thrilled if I ever got a B," Bronco said with a loud laugh.

"Don't you dare," Chad said insistently. "Don't you dare get a B just to make Tess and Julian happy."

"That's right," Bronco said. "I don't want to hear Tess give a graduation speech about her daddy the lawyer and the need to walk all over people to get ahead."

"That's right," Chad said. "I'd much rather hear what you'd have to say. Besides, think how dramatic it would be. You hardly talk to anybody for four years, and then you put it all out there in one speech."

"Yeah," Bronco agreed. "Chad and I will cheer for you."

"You might be the only ones who would," Megan said.

"Aren't we enough?" Bronco asked.

"Yes," Megan answered after a pause for reflection. "You two are enough, and you're more than I've had up until now."

Bronco got up and went to where Megan's books were stacked on the table. "Here," he said, picking them up and handing them to her. "Maybe you'd better study a little."

Megan smiled, and opened one of her notebooks.

Chapter 23

"Is everybody finished?" Chad asked.

Affirmative answers came from both corners, and everyone went back to their previous chairs at the table as if they had assigned seats.

"Well?" Chad asked with a smile. "How did it go?"

"I have to admit it wasn't as dumb an idea as I thought at first," Mel said.

"It was very enlightening," Julian said.

"I wouldn't want to do it every day," Marcus said, "but it was definitely cool this once."

"Good," Chad said, "because there is one more step in the process."

"Spare us," Tess said. "You've pushed us far enough."

"Don't you even want to hear what the last step is?" Chad asked.

"I do," Bronco said.

"The last step, after a group has finished its work, should be to celebrate," Chad announced. "So now we need to celebrate."

"Great idea," Bronco said, "but how? I mean, we don't exactly have the right party ingredients here."

"Sure we do," Chad said. "We have each other."

"And we have music," Julian added quickly before someone mocked Chad.

"That's right," Mel said. "I have some fine celebration music right here."

"And here's my player," Julian said, shoving it down the table to her.

Mel looked through her tapes, picked one, and put it in. A few seconds later, music blared.

"What is that?" Julian asked.

"The latest from one of my favorite groups," Mel said. "Don't you know anything?"

"Must have missed them," Julian muttered.

The lyrics filled the room.

When I wake up in the morning
Ooh baby, baby
Against your sweaty back
I want to keep you always
But you just turn away.
When I wait for you at night
Ooh baby, baby
All you want from me
Is my sexy appetite.
Ooh baby, baby
Ooh baby, baby
Ooh baby, baby
Be my sweaty lover tonight.

"What profound poetry," Tess said with a frown.

"Lyrics to listen to with that perfect someone special," Julian said with a snort. "And people say they aren't writing them like they used to."

"So what do you want, Frank Sinatra or Barry Manilow or something?" Mel snapped. "Besides, this isn't music to listen to. This is music to dance to."

"Let's dance," Chad said.

Everyone stared at him.

"Dancing's a fine celebration," he said. "Come on. Get up and dance."

"Well, it might help us drown out the lyrics," Julian said, holding out his hand to Tess.

She looked at the hand as if it held a knife ready to stab her. "You want me to dance?"

"Why not?" Julian said. "Chad's gotten us this far. We may as well trust him on this one, too."

Reluctantly Tess got out of her chair. Julian formally held out his arms, taking Tess' right hand in his left, and putting his right arm gingerly around her. They stood frozen, like two children being forced to take dancing lessons. Finally they began to move stiffly, at least two feet between their bodies.

"That's pitiful," Mel said. "Let's show them how to do it." She pulled Marcus from his chair and plastered her body against his. He quickly got the idea, and they began moving to the music.

"You don't dance like a virgin," Marcus whispered in Mel's ear.

"And you don't dance like a hardware salesman," Mel whispered back.

"Megan?" Chad asked. "Shall we?"

Megan gave him a very hesitant look but got to her feet.

"Stand behind the chair," Chad said. "I'll lead."

Megan leaned against the back of his chair, and Chad used the electric switch to move forward, then backward, to the beat of the music.

Once again it was Bronco who was left alone. Chad and Megan danced their way over to him.

"Ask her to dance," Megan leaned down to whisper.

"Cut in on Marcus," Chad suggested, then took Megan away.

Bronco sat, his fists clenched, his eyes glued on the undulating bodies of Mel and Marcus. Finally he bounded out of his chair and stomped across the room. He came up behind Marcus and tapped him on the shoulder. Marcus whirled, saw Bronco, and let go of Mel. Bronco reached out his arms to the surprised Mel and was just ready to put them around her when the door from the hallway slammed back against the wall.

"What is the meaning of this?" Mr. Waldo bellowed.

Julian pounced on the tape player and silenced the music.

"We were cele . . . dancing," Chad said with quiet dignity.

"I can see you were dancing, but what makes you think you had my permission to do that?" Mr. Waldo yelled.

Miss Bitterman had come in behind him. "Mr. Waldo," she began. "These kids haven't had a very pleasant day cooped up in here, so if they can find a way to have some fun . . ."

"Since when has school been about having fun?" Mr. Waldo bellowed, clutching his stomach.

"Certainly not since you've been around," Bronco muttered.

"Mr. Waldo," Chad said, "I have a complaint."

"Yes, yes, what is it?" Mr. Waldo said. "Make it short. I haven't got time for this."

"You gave the whole school a chance to turn in information about the spray-painting and get a reward. I think we should have an equal chance."

"I have given you people chance after chance to tell me the truth, and you have not done it," Mr. Waldo yelled.

"I think you should give us one more chance,"

Chad said, while the rest looked at him in amazement except for Megan, who was once again sitting with her head bowed low.

"All right," Mr. Waldo said, "but I warn you. My patience has been exhausted. There better not be any more of your games. Miss Bitterman, give them each a sheet of paper."

Miss Bitterman scurried to unlock her office, get paper, and hand it out.

"Give them to Miss Bitterman when you're done," Mr. Waldo said, thudding to his office where he unlocked the door and slammed it behind him.

Chad looked from Bronco to Tess to Julian to Mel to Marcus to Megan. "Remember everything you've learned," he said.

Chapter 24

Tense silence filled the room. Nobody wrote; nobody moved. Finally Megan broke the spell as her pen began to move across the sheet of paper in front of her.

"Don't you dare," Bronco hissed at her.

Megan looked up at him, smiled tentatively, and then bent down to her paper again.

"Megan," Marcus hissed at her, glancing to see if Miss Bitterman was paying attention. "Megan."

Megan lowered her head still further.

Finally, everyone began to write, Tess with a frown, Marcus with a grin. Miss Bitterman hovered around the table, taking each paper as it was completed.

"I hope Mr. Waldo finds these helpful," she said without much optimism in her voice.

"He will," Bronco said, handing her his paper.

"Sure will," Marcus added, holding out his.

"I think so, too," Mel said, giving puzzled glances to both Bronco and Marcus.

"Will you take this before I change my mind," Tess snapped, causing Julian to stare at her.

"Finished!" Chad announced with pleasure.

"Here is mine, completed in style," Julian said, signing his with a flourish.

Megan didn't say anything, and Miss Bitterman took her paper without comment.

There seemed to be a collective sigh of relief as Miss Bitterman knocked on the door and then entered Mr. Waldo's office.

"This should all be over soon," Tess said finally.

"You didn't get Megan in trouble, did you?" Chad asked tentatively.

"Now what do you think?" Tess snapped.

"I'm not sure," Chad replied, and nobody else seemed to be willing to take a guess, either. Actually, none of them had much time to ponder.

"I've had it with you disrespectful, lying, irresponsible adolescent criminals!" Mr. Waldo screamed as he threw open his office door and came hurtling into the room.

"Hold on, now," Bronco said. "I confessed. I thought you'd be the happiest man in the world now that you could nail me again."

"You are making a mockery of the concept of justice!" Mr. Waldo screamed. "But I'll make you pay. I'm charging all of you with insubordination, with disruption of the orderly educational process, and with anything else I can think of. I'll make you sorry you ever decided to trifle with me." The veins in his temples pulsed as if they were living snakes, and his entire body trembled.

"I confessed!" Bronco screamed back at him. "What is your problem, man? Here, lock me up. Take me away. Make yourself happy!"

"Shut up!" Mr. Waldo screamed, throwing the stack of papers in his hand onto the table. "I hope you are enjoying your little game, because it's over now."

Seven puzzled faces stared at the apoplectic assistant principal.

"Mr. Waldo," Miss Bitterman began.

"Shut up!" Mr. Waldo screamed.

"Now don't you yell at her," Bronco said with a snarl.

"This needs to stop," Miss Bitterman said plaintively.

While the argument raged, Julian picked up the papers from the table. He quickly read through them, disbelief building on his face. At the first pause in the noise, he began to read out loud.

" 'I did it. I spray-painted the building because I don't like you. There. Go ahead and call my parents. They think you're a weenie, too. Eddie Bronco Broncoman.' "

"I told you I confessed," Bronco shouted. "And you're an even bigger weenie than I thought you were."

Julian quickly cut off Bronco before he could elaborate any further and read the next paper. " 'I confess to the spray-painting of the front of Conroy High. I did it because of intense academic pressure which led to temporary insanity and a mild case of amnesia covering the period of time when I committed the crime; therefore, I cannot be held fully accountable and should be given help rather than punishment. Julian Bond Thompson.' "

"You confessed, too?" Bronco asked in amazement.

"Oops," Julian said with a smile.

"Mockery!" Mr. Waldo shouted.

" 'I confess to the vandalism on the front of the building,' " Julian read from the next paper. " 'Since your investigation led to no concrete evidence, and since the conditions under which I have been held constitute undue punishment, and since I am a minor governed by the Code of Conduct, and since I will have professional legal representation, your case against me is not a particularly strong one. Perhaps you would be advised to seek restitution with no indication on my permanent record. Tess Eisman.' "

"I'm sorry, Tess," Chad said. "I'm sorry I doubted you."

Tess raised her chin and looked at him with something that strongly resembled pride.

" 'I did it, man, but only because you are decidedly uncool. You could help your reputation around this place if you took it easy on me. Peace. Love. Marcus Duke.' "

"See what I mean?" Mr. Waldo said. "See what I mean about this? Obviously you planned this to make me look like a fool."

"We didn't plan it," Bronco said. "We just accidentally made you look like a fool."

" 'I spray-painted the building,' " Julian read. " 'You may have my full and complete cooperation if you don't try to find out who gave me the auditorium key. I will take whatever punishment you deem fair as long as I am the only one punished. Megan Massapalo.' "

"Deals?" Mr. Waldo sputtered. "You think any of you are in a position to make deals with me?"

"Looks that way," Bronco said with a pleased smile.

" 'Okay,' " Julian read from the next paper in the stack, " 'I did it. School was boring today, and it needed something to liven it up. When people want to be entertained, you know who they turn to, and I couldn't let my admirers down. Mel Savage.' "

"You confessed, too?" Bronco asked her in amazement.

"What, you think you're the only one with a conscience?" Mel asked him.

"Conscience? How can any of you use that word?" Mr. Waldo yelled. "You're a pack of liars, that's what you are."

"Uncool," Marcus proclaimed with a shake of his head. "Definitely way uncool."

" 'I confess,' " Julian read from the last paper. " 'I needed to let people know that the handicapped are real human beings who break rules and do things others think they can't. I'm sorry if you got hurt in the process, Mr. Waldo. Chad Rheingard.' "

"Fine," Mr. Waldo said. "This is just fine. What am I supposed to do with seven confessions?"

"It worked," Chad said in amazement. "It actually worked. I hoped it might, but I didn't really believe it would."

"What worked?" Bronco asked him, ignoring Mr. Waldo, who was pacing frantically back and forth.

"Telling secrets, celebrating together," Chad said. "It's supposed to make people care about each other, have some kind of identity as a group. I just never thought it would work this well."

"Did you ever think that some of us might have confessed out of desperate need to get away from this group?" Tess asked, but Chad just smiled.

"And I did it to impress Marcus," Mel said, leaning toward him. Bronco growled softly.

"Seven," Mr. Waldo bellowed. "I want one confession, and I've got seven. What am I supposed to do with seven confessions?" He seemed to no longer be aware of his audience; instead, he was completely involved in his own hysteria.

"Why don't you consider us all guilty?" Julian suggested. "We all confessed, so divide the punishment among us. Why don't you suspend each of us for a day, and we'll split the cost of cleaning off the spray-paint. Isn't that fair?"

"As long as it doesn't go on our permanent records," Tess insisted.

"And instead of calling in everyone's parents, why don't you just call in mine? They haven't been here for a few months, and they'd probably like to catch up on what's been going on," Bronco suggested.

"You're all willing to take the blame?" Miss Bitterman suddenly asked, looking from one to another. "Every one of you?"

They all nodded.

"Haven't we made that clear?" Julian asked. "Here are our confessions."

"Just call us the Conroy Seven," Chad said with a grin.

"You won't think this is all such a game when I'm through with you," Mr. Waldo said grimly.

"Stop it," Miss Bitterman said, whirling to face the red-faced Mr. Waldo. "Stop treating these kids like they're common criminals."

"What would you call them?" Mr. Waldo fussed, swerving around her to continue pacing.

"I think they're wonderful," Miss Bitterman said, her voice trembling.

"Wonderful?" Mr. Waldo snarled, stopping inches away from her. "Wonderful? They wreak havoc with the building, and with my good name, and you call them wonderful? They're hooligans, that's what they are."

"Stop it right now," Miss Bitterman said with surprising force.

"Since when do you give me orders, Miss Bitterman?" Mr. Waldo asked.

"There's something you need to know," she said.

Chapter 25

"Whatever it is, Miss Bitterman, it will simply have to wait," Mr. Waldo said firmly. "Can't you see that I have enough to deal with here?"

"No," Miss Bitterman insisted. "You have to hear this right now."

"All right," Mr. Waldo sighed. "Come into my office."

"No," Miss Bitterman said. "I want them to hear this, too."

"You are trying my patience, Miss Bitterman," Mr. Waldo said, resuming his pacing.

"I don't know quite how to say this," she began.

"Just say it, and say it quickly," Mr. Waldo said, spinning on his heel to pace in the opposite direction.

"I spray-painted the building," Miss Bitterman said softly, her eyes on the floor.

"What?" Mr. Waldo said, wheeling in amazement. "Another confession? What is this, communal confession day? I've already got seven useless confessions. How many more do you think I need?"

"I'm serious," Miss Bitterman stated flatly. "I did it."

"Now, Miss Bitterman," Bronco said with a

chuckle, "what are you saying that for? You would never do a thing like that."

"I did it," she repeated.

"What are you trying to prove?" Mr. Waldo asked, a whine in his voice. "Why are you joining these hooligans in tormenting me?"

"Wait. I can prove it," Miss Bitterman suddenly announced. She raced over to her desk, crawled over it, and opened the deep side drawer. Triumphantly she pulled something out, crawled back over the desk, and rejoined the now stationary Mr. Waldo. "Here. Now do you believe me?" She thrust into his hand a can of red spray paint.

"What are you doing with this?" Mr. Waldo asked, his voice shaky.

"I used it this morning," Miss Bitterman announced. "See? Now you have to believe me and let these kids go."

Bronco let out a loud whoop. "I can't believe it!" he said jubilantly. "You blamed us, and an *adult* did it. Not only that, an adult who works for you! Who's the weenie now, Mr. Waldo?"

The rest of the kids seemed too stunned to react.

"Why?" Mr. Waldo asked plaintively. "Why did you turn on me, too?"

"I did it because I care about you," Miss Bitterman said simply.

"Ooooh," Mel said suggestively. "You care about him? How much do you care?"

"You care about Mr. Waldo?" Bronco said in complete disbelief.

"I care about him very much," Miss Bitterman said with quiet dignity, her cheeks blushing red.

Mr. Waldo was speechless, staring at Miss Bitterman.

"So if you care about him, strange as that is, why

did you spray-paint that he is a weenie on the front of the building for all the world to see?" Bronco asked.

"I was trying to save him," Miss Bitterman said.

"Save me? Save me? Save me from what?" Mr. Waldo sputtered back to life.

"From yourself," Miss Bitterman responded.

"By humiliating me?" Mr. Waldo asked.

"He has a point there," Marcus said.

"I tried all the quiet ways," Miss Bitterman said with more spirit in her voice. "You wouldn't listen to me."

"Perhaps we should discuss this in my office," Mr. Waldo said, suddenly aware of the seven pairs of eyes glued to the action.

"No," Miss Bitterman said with determination. "You brought these kids into the middle of this, and now they deserve to hear the truth."

"That's only fair," Julian said, leaning back as if waiting for the movie to begin.

"What you don't know," Miss Bitterman said, speaking to the students rather than to Mr. Waldo, "is that I was one of Mr. Waldo's students right here at Conroy High years ago when he was just starting out."

"I fail to see the relevance of this," Mr. Waldo interrupted.

"Let her talk," Bronco said, and Mr. Waldo sputtered and paced away.

"He was a great teacher," Miss Bitterman continued. "I know you might find that hard to believe, but he was."

Mr. Waldo made a strangling sound and paced faster. Bronco smiled.

"He really cared about his students, wanted them to learn, went out of his way to help them."

144

"This is the same Mr. Waldo?" Bronco asked. "Are you sure?"

"Yes," Miss Bitterman said firmly. "The same one."

"So what happened to him?" Bronco asked.

"Next he became a counselor," she continued. "By the time I finished school, got my secretarial training, and came back here to work, he had switched to guidance."

"Is that when he . . . changed?" Julian asked.

"No," Miss Bitterman said. "He was a good counselor, too. I always used to hear kids say that he was fair, and that he was always willing to listen to them. Kids that didn't even have him as their advisor used to stop by just to talk to him."

"Are you sure you're not exaggerating, Miss Bitterman?" Bronco asked.

"No," she answered firmly.

Mr. Waldo paced; the kids were focusing so intently on Miss Bitterman's story they almost forgot he was there.

"So what happened next?" Chad asked.

"Then he became an administrator," Miss Bitterman said. "That's when it all started. He wanted to be good at his job, just like he always had been, and somewhere along the way, being a good administrator made him lose touch with the kids. He started to focus on the trouble they created rather than the good they did. Then the kids started to dislike him, and he started to dislike the kids, and look at the results."

Everyone's eyes darted to the pacing Mr. Waldo, who seemed to not even be listening.

"He's going to kill himself with that stomach ulcer he has, or have a stroke or a heart attack or something," Miss Bitterman said fiercely. "I've told him over and over again to slow down, to look on the bright side, to go back to what he's good at, but he won't."

"So you spray-painted the building to get his attention," Bronco said.

"Yes," she said. "I guess it was a stupid thing to do, but I was desperate. I thought it would make him stop and take a good look at the position he's in. I even thought maybe the principal would reassign him to a different job, and then he'd be happy again."

"You really do care about him, don't you?" Mel asked in an astonished voice.

"Yes," Miss Bitterman said. "You may not believe this, but I did it out of love."

"Cool," Marcus announced.

Mr. Waldo stopped his pacing and stared at Miss Bitterman.

"I suppose you hate me now," she said to Mr. Waldo.

He stared for a moment longer, then spun on his heel to resume pacing.

"I thought no one would have to know who did it," Miss Bitterman said, looking at the kids. "I knew I wouldn't be suspected. I used my keys to get into the custodians' quarters and then up through the access stairs to the roof."

"But then we got called in," Julian said.

"Yes, and even then I thought Mr. Waldo would figure out that none of you had done it, and you wouldn't be in any trouble, and I could keep my secret."

"But he wouldn't believe us," Tess said in an accusing voice with the emphasis on "he."

"No," Miss Bitterman said sadly. "The old Mr. Waldo would have believed you, but not the way he is now."

"So what made you finally decide to tell?" Chad asked.

"All of you," she said. "You all were sticking together, trying to keep each other out of trouble, and I couldn't let you take the blame for something I did."

"He should have listened to us the first time," Bronco said.

"Actually, I'm glad it turned out this way," Miss Bitterman said. "I'm a rotten criminal, and I would have been scared every minute that someone was going to find out the truth." She waited until Mr. Waldo paced by her, and then she put out her hand to stop him. "If you want me to quit, I will," she said quietly to him. "If you hate me, I'll understand. I just hope you'll think about being what you're meant to be, what you're happy doing, and that isn't hating kids."

Mr. Waldo refused to meet her eyes. He headed for his office and softly, quietly, pulled the door closed behind him.

Miss Bitterman sank into an empty chair at the table and buried her face in her hands.

"I think you're great," Bronco said, edging his chair over next to hers.

"I'm sorry for everything you all have been through today," her muffled voice said.

"That's okay," Julian reassured her. "It certainly has been a change in the routine."

"Are we free to leave now?" Tess asked.

With that, the dismissal bell rang. The seven gathered together their belongings and walked out without a word. The most unusual Friday in all their years of school was finally over, and it had left them speechless.

Chapter 26

Julian, Tess, Marcus, Mel, Bronco, and Megan all received mysterious phone calls from Chad over the weekend. "Meet me in the front lobby before homeroom on Monday," was all that he would say. He didn't wait for an answer.

Bronco was the first to arrive, soon followed by Mel. Bronco stood awkwardly, staring at Mel's outfit. This time she had on black stretch pants that fit like a second layer of skin, and a bright blue sweater.

"Isn't that a little bright for Monday morning?" Bronco finally said.

"Nobody else has complained," Mel said, flinging back her hair.

"I'm not complaining," Bronco said. "You look . . ."

Before he could complete the sentence, Marcus arrived, skateboard in hand. "What's up?" he asked.

"Beats me," Bronco answered.

Julian was next, soon followed by Tess, who stood off from the rest. They watched as a van pulled up in front of the school, a ramp descended, and Chad and his wheelchair emerged. The van pulled away, and Chad's wheelchair whirred up the ramp to the right of the school's steps. Bronco held open the door for him.

"Where's Megan?" were Chad's first words.

"We don't know," Julian said.

"I need for everyone to be here," Chad said insistently.

"Want me to go look for her?" Julian asked.

"Would you?" Chad said.

Julian turned to go, only to find that Megan was standing silently off to the side, hidden by the crowds of students entering the building.

"Great!" Chad said when he saw Megan. "Let's go somewhere a little quieter."

The rest followed as he led the way down the first hallway toward the cafeteria. The doors were unlocked, and Chad took them in the cafeteria, away from the building's early morning bustle.

"I have something for each of you," Chad said. "I know that we'll all end up going our separate ways again, but I wanted you to have something to remember Friday by."

Chad reached into a bag in his lap. "Bronco, this is yours," he said.

Bronco took what Chad offered and unfolded a large, pale blue T-shirt. On the front, in large black letters, was "The Conroy Seven." On the back, in more large black letters, was "Free at Last."

"This is great," Bronco said. He immediately stripped off the black T-shirt he was wearing, flexed his muscles in Mel's direction, and put on his new shirt. He modeled the shirt for the others, who laughed appreciatively.

"What's that?" Julian asked, pointing to the upper right side of Bronco's shirt. The rest gathered around as Bronco craned his head down to check.

There, carefully hand-drawn in different colored markers, was a caricature of Bronco, muscles bulging, face smiling. His hand was reaching for a fire

149

alarm, and above the alarm, like a genie coming out of a bottle, was Mr. Waldo's face.

"Did you draw that?" Mel asked.

"Yes," Chad said.

"That's great!" Marcus said.

"Thank you," Chad said simply.

"Are you accusing me of pulling that fire alarm?" Bronco said with a smiling snarl.

"You're just near it. Your hand isn't actually touching," Chad said with a laugh.

"Still, if Mr. Waldo is around, you'd better cover that up," Julian said.

Chad reached into his bag again and handed Marcus a shirt. His had the same Conroy Seven logo, and everyone, even Tess, hovered around to see what his drawing was. Chad had drawn Marcus on his skateboard, bangs hanging in his eyes, arms outstretched. He was poised at the edge of a cliff, a path winding down it.

"Did I make it?" Marcus asked Chad.

"Absolutely," Chad answered.

"Thanks," Marcus said. "This is totally cool." He took off a shirt emblazoned with skating logos and put on Chad's gift.

"You don't fill it out quite as well as I do, but it looks good," Bronco said.

"Mel," Chad said, checking out the next shirt.

Mel's picture had her dressed in black with spiked heels and lots of jewelry.

"You got her right," Bronco said.

"Look carefully," Chad said. "Right over her head."

"Now why'd you put a halo there?" Mel asked.

"Because you're not as tough as you want people to think," Chad said with a smile.

"I like it," Mel said after a moment's thought, giving Chad a puzzled smile, wondering how much he knew.

"Put it on," Bronco said. "You have to, right now."

"We won't look," Marcus added.

"No way," Mel said. "I'll be right back." She ducked behind a serving counter at the front of the cafeteria and emerged with sweater in hand, T-shirt on.

"Julian's is next," Chad announced. Loud laughter greeted his picture, and even Tess had to join in. Julian was pictured behind the wheel of a car. Off to the side was another car stuck in mud. Under Julian's car was one simple word—"Oops."

"I deserved that," Julian said with a smile. He unbuttoned his oxford cloth shirt and tucked his new shirt into his gray dress pants.

Tess' was next. Somehow Chad had managed to picture Tess as a perfect ice sculpture.

"The ice maiden," Julian said with a smile.

"But she's melting," Chad said.

Sure enough, tiny drips ran all the way down the front of Tess' shirt.

"Thank you," Tess said. She went behind the counter and emerged wearing the shirt with her navy pleated wool skirt.

"Sure it won't ruin your reputation to let people know there's a heart in there?" Julian asked.

Tess smiled in return.

"What about you?" Bronco suddenly asked Chad. "Don't you have one?"

Chad unzipped the jacket he was wearing, revealing his own shirt. On it, he was standing upright, arms extended. Coming to meet him, arms also extended, was a model that would do any centerfold proud.

"At least I can dream," Chad said. Then, before

the mood could become somber, he took out the last shirt. "Megan," he said.

She stepped forward. Again, the group gathered to study Chad's artwork. Tess' gasp was the first reaction, followed by Julian's matching gasp. Chad had drawn Megan at a podium, dressed in the traditional cap and gown of graduation. The numbers "4.0" were written under the podium.

Megan pulled the shirt on over the white blouse she was wearing.

Before Tess and Julian had regained their power of speech, the warning bell for homeroom rang.

"Better go," Chad said with a smile. "We wouldn't want to get in any trouble today."

Megan followed Chad's wheelchair out, leaning down to whisper to him. Marcus went with them, clapping Chad on the back. Bronco walked beside Mel, and right when they got to the doorway, he started talking to her. Tess and Julian remained frozen in place, staring at each other.

JANE MCFANN has written a number of books for young adults including *One Step Short*. She lives in Newark, Delaware, where she is a high school English teacher.